Harry Croft

Harry Croft

Back To RETRO JUSTICE

Max Barrington

Etteleah

CONTENTS

Harry Croft

When Harry's beloved wife is taken from him through reckless youths in a stolen car, he decides to reinstate justice the way it was when he was a police sergeant many years before.

Dedicated to my loving wife Lynette

This book is a work of fiction. Unless otherwise indicated, all the names, characters, businesses, places, events and incidents in this book are either the product of the author's imagination or used in a fictitious manner. Any resemblance to actual persons, living or dead, or actual events and/or places is purely coincidental.

Max Barrington

Harry Croft

'What the fuck do you mean when you say that I can't work here any more lad, I've bin here since well before you were born' said Harry, or 'Aitch' as all his workmates called him, in his very strong Scouse, or Liverpool accent that he had not lost in the fifty-five years that he had been in Australia.

'It's not my idea Harry, it's the insurance company, they won't insure you for workers compensation because you are now sixty five years old', Simon Drury was trying to explain to Harry Croft the district manager at the south side maintenance depot in the ACT.

'I put you into that fucking job lad, you fucking arse wipe and you have turned into the biggest fucking arse licker and crawler that mankind has ever ad the misfortune of coming across, now crawl back to your little arse licking office with your cock sucking buddies and leave me alone.'

Sadly, Simon had to call the police in to remove Harry Croft from his office. Harry had been the district manager of that depot for the last twenty five years, he was now past the age where he could be covered by workers' compensation, so in accordance with local government policy, he needed to retire. Simon knew that financially Harry was fine with his super and he would be eligible for an age pension, sadly Harry could not see all the benefits that retiring had to offer.

The police entered Harry's office without knocking, a big mistake,

'Who the fuck do you pricks think you are and what, the fuck are you doing in here'

'Sorry sir, but we have orders to remove you from these premises and with reasonable force if required', said the first class constable who had entered the office with a female constable.

Harry started to cool down, he realised that these people were only doing their jobs and it didn't matter what he thought about the system there was nothing he could do about it, plus the fact that he didn't want to make a complete fool of himself.

'Just give me ten minutes son, and I'll get out of your way'. Harry went into the store room and found an empty carton and went back to his office to pack the few things he had in and on his desk, he had a few books on the bookcase which he also took, there were some other books that he decided to leave there.

It had taken him no longer than five minutes and Harry was in the car park with his cardboard box, and then he realised that he only had his govy there, he put his cardboard box down onto the bonnet of the car, a Toyota Corolla poverty pack as Harry called it, Harry took his mobile telephone from his trouser pocket and looked for Simon Drury in his contacts then pushed the button.

'You ok Harry, sorry about all this mate."

'I'm sorry Simon, I just lost it, It's just a shock to me is all I can say', Harry said, although he had known for months that yesterday was his deadline and the last possible day that he could remain in the employment of the department. 'Look I ave only govy car to get home, I'll drop it back tomorrow an', Simon cut him off.

'Just bring it to the Canberra Club on Friday night where your farewell dinner is and leave it in the basement car park and I'll get it sorted from there.'

Harry's wife Val, wasn't surprised to see him come home at ten thirty that Thursday morning. She had warned him this morning before he had left to go to work that he was wasting his time going and that she didn't think that they would even let him in the door, he was being just too obstinate, bloody old fool.

'Did they give you that car as a going away present? Or did you knock it off, Harry'?

Harry didn't answer her but went to the fridge instead and took out a stubbie of Carlton draught and just muttered something that was totally beyond any resemblance to the English language and went into the lounge and sat to drink his beer and read the Canberra Times. After about an hour he wandered back into the kitchen where Val wasn't really doing anything, Harry looked around the kitchen as he was sort of hoping that a bit of lunch might have been happening. At this time at work, he would be at the takeaway that was beside the depot and wondering what to have for lunch, it was always either a pie and hot chips, or fish and chips, or sometimes chicken and chips but it was always 'and chips' and he would take it back to the depot and sit in the lunch room with all his workmates to eat his lunch.

The conversation in the lunch room was about the shit food that they had bought from next door and they all agreed that they would find somewhere else to get lunch from tomorrow, but that never happened.

Harry, after realising that lunch, did not look like it was 'on' in the kitchen, asked Val if she would like to walk up to the Statesman Hotel with him for lunch.

'Are you bored Harry? you have been home for all of one hour and one half and you do not know what to do with yourself' Val asked. 'You get up to the pub and have some lunch there Harry and leave me to my work, go and enjoy yourself'.

And he did go, he wasn't going to, but then he was going to and then he did, so he walked the three hundred metres from their home to the pub. Of course at twelve thirty on a Thursday lunchtime, there was no one there that he knew, they were all at work, there were only old retired blokes and unemployed bludgers, but the place was busy and there was a mixed grill on as today's special which sounded pretty good to Harry, but first a couple of beers at the bar.

'What are you having mate' the barman recognised Harry, 'Day off mate?'

'Would you believe it Wal, I am now officially retired, middy of tooths thanks'

'Holy shit Harry, your not going to be here every day

annoying us are you? Have you plans Harry, are you going to move down the coast and go fishing every day?'

'Mate, I don't even eat fish anymore, so why would I want to go and catch the bastards, cheer's Wal', Harry went to find a table, placed his beer on it then went to the food serverey to order a 'mixed grill'. The young girl serving, who looked like she really did not want to be in the pub working and was doing everyone who ordered a meal, a personal favour.

'You right mate?' She asked Harry. Harry turned and looked behind him, then turned back and spoke to the girl.

'Were you talking to me?', Harry asked with indignation, 'I thought you were talking to a dog'.

'Nah, I was asking what you wanted', Harry just shrugged and could not be bothered, but he made a mental note to tell Nick, the hotel manager about this young lady's attitude.

'I'll have a mixed grill please'

'That's twenty dollars, mate'.

Harry passed the twenty dollars to the girl and said 'Thank you very much, and don't ever call me 'mate' again'.

She just gave him a blank stare as a zombie would, but didn't know any different, it was a waste of words from Harry.

Harry went back to his table only to discover his beer was gone, he looked around, which was useless as almost everyone in there had a middy of beer, either in their hands or sitting in front of them. Harry went to the bar and told Wal that his bar hand was a bit anxious about collecting glasses and must have taken his beer. Wal said that Phil, the roustabout hadn't started yet and suggested that it may have been one of the dole wackers playing pool.

'Don't worry about it Harry, it's not worth it these days, I'll get you another one, back in the old days young pricks like that, I would have thrown through the door with a following boot in their arse and would ban the pricks for a month. If I do that today, those assholes would have me charged for assault'. Then Wal added, 'better get back to your table mate while your meal is still there'.

They both enjoyed a laugh.

Harry arrived back home about an hour after he'd left to go there and Val said to him,

'That didn't work did it, Harry, you don't know what to do with yourself, do you? What are you going to do, you had the chance to think about it six months ago when they told you, but no, that won't happen to me sez Harry and now what? You don't want to go down the coast and get a place near the beach or the river. You will need to work something out, you can't just mope around here like this.

Harry, was just *not* ready to retire, he had completed his apprenticeship as a carpenter at the age of twenty and then had worked on various construction projects at many levels for ten years. At thirty Harry had joined the ACT Police force and had risen to sergeant within ten years but he didn't feel it was really the life for him and left there to take up the advertised position of district manager for the then, Dept of Housing and Construction.

Self Government had come along for the ACT and things changed slightly with Harry's position with the biggest change being that he was given a much bigger salary and a home garaging Government (govy) car.

Harry had decided that he was too young at sixty five to retire and decided to look for some sort of work, maybe just until he got to around seventy five thought Harry. As fate would have it and before Harry had to do any serious thinking about what he should be looking for in a job at his age, he got a call from one of the other DM's (district manager) at another maintenance depot, not really a friend but they both got on well together, and during the conversation, Harry had mentioned that he would most likely try to find some sort of a job. The other DM said that if he was interested he knew of a position going for a maintenance cell supervisor at one of the large private office buildings in the city. Harry reminded him that he was now sixty five and apparently workers' compensation insurance was a problem, whereas his former colleague told him, not in private enterprise. Harry became interested and got the contact details for the position.

Val was quite happy when Harry announced that he intended to apply for the position as a maintenance supervisor with a large company that supplied this type of service on contract, to many private high rise office complexes, and buildings.

Harry had made contact by phone to the contact name he had been provided who in turn did confirm that such a position was indeed available and asked Harry if he could contact the HR manager, make an appointment with him and bring along his CV , he gave Harry a number for HR manager. Harry thanked the person on the other end of the telephone conversation and then hung up.

Harry was a little concerned, he didn't have a CV, as such,

back when he applied for his last job, twenty five years ago it was called a resume and he still had a copy of that, he didn't really have much to add to it though. After a long thinking session with Val, Val suggested that he give Gwen, his former secretary a call and ask her about a CV.

Gwen was so delighted that Harry had rang, she wanted to call him but thought that he may have still have been too upset with all the commotion of him having to leave his job. Harry finally, got around to asking her about a CV and that he had nothing really to add to it as he had only been with his last job for the last twenty five years.

"Harry, I have been with you for eighteen of those twenty five years and in that time you have attended at least six courses where you have received a qualification and one that I know of where you received a degree. Give me an hour or so and I will email a list to you, if you like I will prepare an up to date CV, how would that be?

Within an hour Harry had received to new CV from Gwen, It read like some other, somewhat dignified, persons CV rather than his. True he had not really added much weight to all the courses that his former job had required him to attend and complete and now when he thought about it, one of them was a three year part time course.

Harry had always only really regarded the courses as a source of a getaway, staying at flash hotels and enjoying the free, rather expensive and extensive meals at hotels, not to mention the endless free drinks, or simply a couple of days off from work each week.

He started to read the qualification that he had acquired

whilst in his former position, it was fairly extensive and also seemed quite impressive.

Other than his original former qualification as a journeyman carpenter, Gwen had added Acumen of Business cert IIII, Human Resources Development, Diploma in Management Skills, Diploma in Applied Science Blg, and on and on. After perusing his new CV, Harry now recalled some of the courses, it had been such a long time ago, surely things would have changed so much by now as to make these qualifications obsolete. Anyway, Harry took his new CV with him to his appointment with the HR manager.

He was nothing that Harry had imagined and Harry thought that maybe he was still at school and just here on work experience. The HR manager introduced himself to Harry,

'Joshua Benthall, Harry, pleased to meet you'.

In Harry's experience, people around this age generally addressed Harry as Mr Croft, Harry responded with a 'Good Morning, Josh"

'Joshua, it's Joshua Harry'

'Right, Joshua'

'You have a rather impressive CV Harry, I must say, However, you do realise that we don't really require such qualifications for the position intended, simply your qualification as a carpenter is sufficient, however your strengths are quite apparent through these further education qualifications. Harry, What do you see as your weak point'.

'I don't know that I do have a weak point, Josh..Joshua'.

'Harry, everybody, myself included, has a weak point or weakness, if you prefer, think about it, Harry'.

'Well, I suppose my weak point would have to be my honesty'.

'I don't think that being honest is a weak point, Harry'.

'Well, responded Harry, 'I don't really care what you think, and I did not come here to be belittled by you, now if you have a position for me then tell me so, otherwise we are both wasting our time here this morning'.

Joshua's smugness disappeared instantly, he had been in this position for two months now and he was not prepared for this reaction, from a person seeking employment. His training did not provide for the aggressive behaviour of job seekers but that of a humble and positive nature. He felt a reversal happening and he could not stop it.

'yes,...er,.there is a position available at one of our properties in the centre of civic'

'And what is the role'? Harry asked, 'What is involved and what is the remuneration'?

Joshua, on his back foot now seemed to be going even further back, 'It's a casual rate of sixty dollars per hour, but because of your age, the insurance company place a surcharge against your cover which will reduce the hourly rate to fifty five dollars per hour', he added the last bit somewhat gingerly.

'That will do', said Harry, I can start next Monday, tell me where I have to go, I will be there at nine o'clock'.

Harry had taken over the interview and had awarded himself the position, Joshua had been aware of this and could do nothing to stop it from happening. Quite feebly and almost apologetically, Joshua found himself following Harry's directive and had supplied him with a written format of the address to be at on Monday at nine am as Harry had dictated, he was to meet the engineer in charge there who would advise him further. Joshua had also given Harry employee and tax declaration forms to complete and Harry told Joshua that he would pass these to the engineer on Monday.

'Nothing else you want to tell me', asked Harry pausing for a response from Joshua, who just looked at him quite blankly, so Harry said 'Good day'.

Harry was back at his car when he looked at the documentation that Josh had given him. The address of the maintenance cell was the lower level on the corners of Northbourne Ave (North bound) and Alinga Street. The company name was Combined Programmed Building Maintenance. They had contracts around the city at various locations and operated from this cell, it was Harry's job to run the cell. 'Piece of piss' Harry thought to himself.

Harry had met with the company's chief engineer at nine o'clock on the following Monday who introduced himself to Harry as Malcolm Tate, he took Harry down in the elevator, which needed an access card to access the basement, where the maintenance cell office and workshop is located and introduced him to the other three tradespeople, one carpenter, one electrician and one plumber, as 'meet your new boss Harry'.

'Jim, how are you Harry, I'm your sparky', said a fairly slim but tall and lanky dark haired man in his forties.

'Im a Charlie, please to meet with you, I look after the plumbing', said the plumber, short fat and Italian.

'Roger, Harry, how are you doing', tall and thick set with a moustache and looked authoritative.

'You must be the chippy then', said Harry to Roger as he shook all of their hands.

Malcolm showed Harry to his new office and explained how the computerised maintenance system worked, his role was to physically assess the maintenance requests and to give an indicative estimate for repair costs then create a scope of works and supervise the works. Harry did have a female office assistant named Veronica but she wasn't coming to work today as she was ill. Before Malcolm left Harry as he had other issues to attend to that morning, he gave Harry a keycard for the elevator and the loading dock shutter and also gave Harry his mobile number to contact him for any reason he should need to do so.

Malcolm called out to Roger as he was leaving and asked him to give Harry a tour of the works.

'As soon as you are ready Harry' responded Roger.

Harry said 'Well I have bugger all else to do, let's go!'

Roger showed Harry the other office where Veronica worked, 'when she's here' Roger said with a little sarcasm, then took Harry to the plumbing workshop, a fairly small area of around six metres by eight, Charlie wasn't there.

The electrical workshop was about the same size as the plumbing and Jim was in there setting up a small switchboard, heading in a westerly direction was the carpentry, and joinery workshop which was around two and a half the size of the other workshops. At the western end of the basement was a loading dock with a ramp exiting onto Moore Street, there was sufficient room to park six cars which Harry was quite pleased about as he had left his car, what seemed like miles away that morning for a car park. Back up near Harry's office was the store area's consisting of three separate seven by seven metre lock up stores backing onto the northern end of the basement.

In the centre storeroom on the back, northern wall, was a set of large double doors that were closed with some items leaning on them.

'What's through there?', Harry asked Roger.

'Another set of locked double doors, goes through to the basement of the building next door, the Jolimont Centre I think, I'm not really sure Harry, I have never really been interested'.

Val was happy to hear all about Harry's new job and pleased when he said that he thought it would be quite ok and that he could virtually please himself how many hours a day, or week for that matter, he wanted to work.

'Pretty cruisy and the extra money can be put away to buy a place down the coast for retirement in about five years' Harry had said to Val, 'that'll give us around six hundred thousand extra to add to it'.

Harry was fitting in pretty well with his new role, he found it to be pretty much the same as his old position with the ACT Government, but this was maybe just a bit more involved. Veronica, Harry's assistant seemed a bit dippy to Harry but after a couple of months they were getting on really well and Veronica revealed to Harry that in the two months that he had been running the cell, they had made half as much money again than the previous guy Damien, that was running the cell. Veronica had also let it slip to Harry that Damien was also on a casual rate and was being paid seventy five dollars per hour. This prompted Harry to give his mate Joshua, the HR manager a call.

'Good morning Josh, it's Harry Croft, trust you are well'.

Joshua's mind was starting to recollect the name Harry Croft and he suddenly sat up in his chair as he realised who it was and he frowned at the shortened use of his name.

'What can I do for you Harry?', Joshua said a bit curtly.

'Josh, my boy', said Harry in his well practised, polished style of voice, 'when you selected me as the incumbent for this position, the remuneration of fifty five dollars per hour, was but for a three month probationary period was it not?'

'I can't say offhand Harry, but I don't think so, I'll have to check your file'...........

'No worries Josh, I'll wait', Harry cut Joshua off very quickly so he would be unable to say that he would call Harry back.

'No Harry, there is not any mention of a probationary period, nor any mention of an increase to the remuneration".

'No worries, then that means that there would be no reason to have to wait for an increase in remuneration to seventy dollars per hour?'.

'I am sorry Harry, I don't really understand what you are saying'.

'I am saying, that you can increase my hourly rate from fifty five dollars per hour to seventy dollars per hour, as from next Monday'.

'I don't have the authority to increase your hourly rate Harry,.

'Then I suggest to you Josh, that you put it to whoever the person is that can make this type of adjustment to my hourly rate and get it all together by next Monday, Goodbye Josh'.

Whatever had happened in the interim period between when Harry had called Joshua and Monday morning, Harry had no idea, but he had received a text message from Joshua on Monday morning advising that his rate of pay was now seventy dollars per hour as of today, 'well done Josh', thought Harry and got on with his work.

Veronica had received a maintenance request from the centre next door and had taken the details and had handed them plus the file on the building over to Harry's inbox. Harry had taken it from his inbox sometime later that afternoon and looked at the request that one area in the building at the ground level had moisture forming on the floor.

The following day Harry had visited the next door buildings caretaker and he had shown Harry the area of condensation, it was a very small area, about one metre wide by four metres long on a tiled section. Harry new instantly that it was a dew point cause of condensation, this can generally, only happen when two different temperatures come into contact. As this building, as with many in Canberra, was using a controlled environment system for heating and cooling it meant that the windows in the building were inoperable to stop either cold or hot air entering the building, and as it was now July in Canberra and the system employed was heating the building, then cold air was coming into contact with the hot air from the heating. In this instance, it seemed that below the ground floor slab was a source of cool air within that confine of the condensation.

Harry asked the caretaker how to get to the basement, to which the caretaker responded that there was no basement in this building, well none that he was aware of anyway.

Harry walked around the outside of the building and found on the western wall adjacent to where the condensation was taking place that a surface level vent that had been previously closed off with a one way damper, had somehow now become open to allow air to enter. Being on the west side put it directly into the prevailing winter winds of around twelve kilometres per hour.

A Simple job smiled Harry upon his discovery, the vent damper was replaced later that day and Harry had inspected the section of tiled area the next day to discover that the area was now dry. The caretaker was amazed at Harry's instant investigation and solution to what he had imagined to be quite a major problem. Harry was good at his job and there was little doubting of that.

It was November now and summer was starting to happen, Val had called Harry on his mobile one Friday afternoon to ask him if he could get some steak on his way home from work that evening as she had totally forgotten to get it while she was shopping earlier that day and thought that a bbq might be nice for dinner that evening and that their son Scott and his wife Zoe and the grandson Morgan would be coming.

Harry had finished work early that Friday, as usual and had called at the Statesman hotel for a beer, it was very busy in the bar and Harry saw a couple of his old drinking mates and joined in a couple of beers with them. There was some sort of altercation in the pool table area and one of the bar staff was trying to evict two young fellows from the pub, they didn't look to be aged any more than fifteen. They were refusing to leave the hotel amid the jeers of onlookers and maybe, even some of their mates, the bar assistant was being careful not to touch either of the two to avoid any later claims of assault that could be directed towards him, he had called the police twice now but there had been no attendance as yet by them.

Suddenly one of the youths picked up a ball from the pool table and threw it towards the crowded bar, the pool ball hit a drinker who had his back turned towards the bar as he was just paying for a round of drinks, the ball struck him some-where in the middle of the back of his head. The scream the victim of the pool ball emitted was loud and mournful and caught the attention of everybody in the bar, perfect timing for the two youths to slip outside unnoticed.

The ambulance had arrived and was in the process of removing the victim from the bar when the police, who had been called prior to the throwing of the ball by the bar staff, arrived to look helplessly on.

'Mate we rang you blokes nearly fifteen minutes ago about a couple of young underage pricks that refused to leave, they got the shits and threw a ball at this poor bastard and then they fucked off' said the bar manager Wal.

'What did they look like mate' asked a young female copper with a somewhat smart attitude and strange sounding voice that nineteen year old females seem to display these days.

'And what the fuck do you think they looked like', said Wal who was quite shaken with the event, 'they were wearing those fucking grey or black fucking hoodies that they all fucking wear'.

The other constable with her, a male who looked a bit older but seemed much smarter told her to follow him outside and they would call for backup and do a search of the adjacent shopping centre and then they both left.

Harry, who had witnessed the full event with his drinking buddies, finished his beer and said see you to them and left the hotel to go to the supermarket to get the steak that his wife had asked him to buy on his way home. Inside the supermarket in the lollies and peanut aisle, Harry saw the two youths that had left the pub after one of them had thrown the pool ball, they were laughing and eating a pack of potato chips that each had taken from the shelf.

Harry could not help himself and said to the youths, ' You know that bloke you hit with the pool ball is in a bad way'.

'Who the fuck do you think you are grandpa, fuck off you stupid old cunt before you get the same'. One of the youths said whilst threatening to throw a can of baked beans that he had in his hand at Harry.

Harry had just started his crouch and natural self preservation to hurl himself at the youth holding the can in his hand when both of the constables that Harry had seen in the pub walked into the aisle and called out STOP!....instinctively, Harry stopped, the youths fled.

It was a great bbq, the steaks that Harry had collected from the supermarket, plus all the other condiments that Val had put towards the meal, were just great. Harry had not told anyone about what had happened at the pub, nor what had happened in the supermarket, but he looked at his son and thought thank christ you didn't turn out like those pieces of shit that I saw today, but he knew that would have been impossible because Harry had been his father and had brought up Scott in a way that involved something that is banned today when bringing up children, not just at home, but also in schools, Marshall punishment.

Harry had heard in the news the next day that the fellow in the pub had died from the injury he had received from the pool ball, but that the police had charged two youths aged sixteen and seventeen with his murder, 'well that's good' thought Harry. One month later both the youths were placed on bonds as they had been under the influence of a substance which affected their ability to behave in a normal manner.

Harry could not understand that although an innocent person had been killed for no reason whatsoever, just a thoughtless deliberate act by two children there was no punishment delivered, they had shown no remorse whatsoever, there was no deterrent to any others that may consider similar actions towards their fellow man.

Because nothing happens when you get caught, in their minds, must seem to mean you can do it, you are not allowed to do it, then you will be told not to do it again, but that is about the extent and it does not matter what you did, murder, assault, steal a car, whatever, it's just a game like a video game, you have to start again.

Harry thought that it was also pathetic that these kids that murdered the guy, were also released by a legal representative that the dead guy was also paying towards by the means of taxation, legal aid. The dead guy was also paying towards the psychologist and human rights affiliates that objected to any form of reprimand towards his killers as it may lead to affecting the mental or social way these youths may react later in life, it could fuck their brain in later life, they may become withdrawn and no longer to participate in normal social behavioural activities.

Little thought seems to go to the victim lying dead in the morgue, to the grieving family who have lost their loved father, husband and in many cases, breadwinner. No, all that matters is that these youths don't suffer any mental issues later in life. Unbelievable, and not a good subject to mention to Harry.

Life does go on and Harry was in his office some weeks after the pub incident, Veronica came into his office and showed to him an invoice that had been rejected from being paid by the company for a 'new vent damper' as it was under the wrong asset charge number.

'Ah shit, sorry said Harry, I do remember that, it was the place next door, Veronica looked it up and inserted the correct asset number so that the sub contractor who completed the job could be paid. Harry thought how strange that although his team could have quite easily have repaired that duct damper, because it was classified as HVAC, heating ventilation and air conditioning, and they did not employ a person qualified in such, then it had to out sourced, hmmm, thought Harry, a new way of life. This little incident, not really an incident, just a little error on Harry's behalf, but it brought back to Harry the day he walked around the building next door and found the air vent with the damaged damper. There would be more of those vents around the base of the building next door, their design is to allow the flow of air as in natural ventilation to the basement of the building, but in the in the event of a fire in the basement, then these dampers within the vent are controlled with a thermostatic device and will shut the damper when triggered.

Harry's mind back to that day and he remembered talking to the caretaker of the building who told Harry that there was no basement in that building. There must be a basement Harry thought, hence the ventilation ducts. He then remembered the double set of doors in the centre storeroom just outside his office, Harry got up from his desk and left his office to look inside the centre store, he went to the double doors and they were locked, reaching into his pocket for the master key to the cell that he had been handed by Malcolm Tate and inserting it into the lock and it turned smoothly and unlocked the doors. Harry opened fully both door leaves only to find another double set of doors set at four hundred millimetres back from the first set of doors, this was to allow for the wall thickness. Harry inserted his master key into the lock but although the key would go into the lock, it would not turn to unlock the doors. Harry made a mental note to find his set of hand picks and the lockaid tool that he had at home somewhere and bring them with him tomorrow to allow further exploration into the mysterious, next door basement. Harry then returned to his office and promptly forgot all about the basement and got back into his work, he was really enjoying this new job, no pressure here, Harry thought, as there was with his former role.

Harry had remembered to locate his lock picking tools from his little workshop he had in the garage and he placed them into the glovebox of his car in order to remember to take them to work with him tomorrow.

That evening following dinner, there was more news about more crime around the ACT, especially car theft, it was now the leading crime around Canberra. Harry thought, other than the politicians who were guilty of taking money under false pretences. Harry had called into the Statesman for a drink on his way home that afternoon and had bumped into an old colleague from his police days, Tony Strause, Tony had been a young twenty something constable when Harry was an 'about to retire sergeant' and he had quite a lot of time for Tony back then. Now Tony was and 'about to retire sergeant' at the age of fifty five and confided in Harry that he was setting up a private enquiry agency just for something to do, he gave Harry one of his new business cards and asked him not to show it around for a while until he had left the force. Harry had wished him luck and suggested they get together more often for a drink and a few yarns about the 'good old days'.

Back at work the next day and Harry had taken his lock picking gear, placed in a small bag, into his office for an exploration adventure later that day when everyone else in the office had left. As an afterthought he took the rechargeable torch, that he had discovered in his cupboard when he had first arrived, he searched for it's charger in every drawer and shelf that was in his office but to no avail, he was about to leave the office in search of a charger when he noticed that one was already plugged into a powerpoint near the door. 'Men's look' Val would say to him if he was at home looking for something, Harry thought, then grinned to himself.

It was three o/clock in the afternoon when the last person had left the cell and Harry was also about to leave and go home when the torch plugged into the charger reminded him of his intending adventure, he grabbed the bag containing the lock picks and also took the torch and headed to the centre storeroom. Removing his lockaid tool and a tensioner from the bag, he then attempted to pick the lock, he wasn't an expert at picking locks but he had enjoyed quite considerable success, that was not to be the case to day however, he had already spent about an hour on the lock when he decided that he would go into the carpentry workshop and find a cordless drill and a six millimetre drill bit, he had one last try and he unlocked the door. You couldn't even make this stuff up, Harry thought as he swung the operable door leaf in towards the pitch black of the mysterious basement.

Shining the torch through the doorway revealed a concrete masonry wall about one point eight meters from the doorway, a corridor Harry thought, the wall went from slab to soffit and was the entire width of the basement, to the right it went for about twelve metres then terminated at the end of the building, to the left it went about twenty five metres and also terminated at the end of the building, but then Harry could just see something along the wall to his left about twenty meters away that had caused a reflection, it looked like a door.

Harry walked through the doorway to his left with the torch beam on the wall, as he approached the reflected item he saw that it was a door, not a normal door but a steel door. It was a flat door with two hinge straps, top and bottom running full width from the hinges on the left of the door, there was a single keyhole escutcheon on the right hand side approximately in the centre between the top and bottom of the door with a single latch lever.

Harry shone his torch on the door thinking that this is the end of my excursion, he took hold of the latch handle and pushed it down expecting it to be solid, the handle moved down, the latch was withdrawn inside the steel door allowing Harry to pull the door towards him, leaving the heavy door open. Harry walked cautiously through the doors opening shining his torch quickly from side to side and wishing that he had someone with him, Harry was feeling quite anxious, most likely because what he had found so far was totally unexpected. He was in another corridor and the walls here were also concrete masonry and painted a dark grey, the floor was smooth concrete and the ceiling was metal, pressed metal Harry guessed as he walked very slowly forward, the corridor abruptly ended with a sharp turn to the right and another door that was wide open, this door seemed to be the same as the door he had entered from the corridor. He was in some sort of reception room with a large barred window beside another door to his left.

Harry's torch gave a single flicker then went out without any other warning, the darkness was indescribable. Harry had made a big mistake when the light went out, he had turned around to look behind him, apparently a quite normal re-action when suddenly you are enveloped into darkness, none-theless a big mistake for Harry as he did not now know which way he was facing. Harry put his hand into his side pocket to retrieve his phone, not there, Hmm it's on the desk he remem-bered, he held out his left arm fully stretched in front of him and walked slowly until he arm touched a wall, or something, he knew that he wanted to find the doorway that he had just entered which, according to Harry's inbuilt compass, meant following this wall to the left, slowly letting his fingers follow the wall until they came to a doorframe, he now knew exactly where he was, he was now leaving the reception area and into the short corridor that would lead to the first steel door, then he would go left and should then see the light from the store-room that he had entered from, did he leave that door open? Anyway, he was doing just fine he thought, until he walked into something just below knee height which caused him to fall forward and over an object that really hurt his knees and his head made contact with what he thought was a low shelf.

Startled and bleeding from his head wound Harry felt around at what he seemed to be suspended on and after some time realised that it must be a toilet pan that his knees were now resting on and that it felt like a wash basin that he had struck with his head. He was lost, what a startling realisation it was to Harry, 'I'm fucking lost' he said to no one and Harry then started to feel frightened, he didn't want to keep walking in the dark because he had no idea of what he may walk into, go back! He thought, I must just now go back away from these things, trying to remember that he came through a door just before he fell, wrong fucking door he thought and grinned as he remembered for some strange reason a joke about a Chinese bookshop, 'Wong fukin bookshop', why would he think about such a stupid thing like that at a time like this, as he was feeling the wall with one hand but now putting his legs forward much more cautiously than before. Then Harry felt another doorway and after feeling all around it decided the door was open and that this must be the exit to the second corridor and he started to move much more confidently and quicker and he knew he must now go to the left of this doorway to reach the corner to the left, yes left, or was it right, no definitely left. Harry had to stop and regain his bearings if he could. He had come through the storeroom door and turned to the left, the first steel door was along that corridor on the right hand side and it led straight forward, then it turned to the right and another doorway, he went through this and then blackness,...think...think. How the fuck did I fall over a toilet, I must have gone to the right, there was a window and a door to the left, but no toilet.......I must have gone right. Wait...which way did I turn when the light went out, left or right...left or right.......any other situation you'd laugh,...fifty fifty, ok if I did turn to the right, when I found the wall I went to the left,....so now,... go right, keep going, keep going, keep going, like the breathalyser show, keep going, another door frame, the door is open, no go left, yes left, keep going, keep going keep going, another door frame, door is open,........let, yes left,.....light, there is light....walk to the light. He was at the store room and he was as shaky as a shit house rat, Harry was a wreck.

Harry went to the bathroom and got a shock when he saw his head, the blood had run down one side of his head onto his neck and onto his white shirt, fark me, unbelievable. Harry looked at this watch, it was almost seven o'clock. He went back to the store and to the double door in the corridor and closed them, he didn't lock them and then he closed the set of doors on the store side and locked these. He no longer had the torch and he decided that he must have dropped that when he fell, must get another torch he thought, two torches he decided as he made his way home.

'Overstayed at the pub' said Val, then seeing the blood on Harry's shirt, "My god Harry, what has happened to you, here sit here and I'll get something'.

'I'm fine...fine, really it's nothing, really I am good'

'Oh my god Harry, what is it what's going on', said Val whilst getting some water water and detol.

'I only tripped in the car park at the pub, some dick must have dropped his tow bar and I didn't see it'.

Harry was thinking, what a dumb thing to say, someone dropped his tow bar. It was the first thing that came to mind, fortunately Val must have been too concerned with all the blood on his shirt to realise what he had said. Val had bathed his cut, it wasn't bad at all, just one of those that tend to make a mess, they had dinner and watched a bit of television and went to bed, all back to normal. Except Harry could not sleep, what the fuck was in the basement next door to them, he was anxious for tomorrow to arrive so he could do some investigating.

It was a great spring Friday morning in Canberra, except

it was bitterly cold and pissing down with rain, Harry's car was booked in for a service at the dealership in Phillip. He had dropped the car off and had decided to walk down to the Woden bus interchange where he would catch a bus into the city centre, civic as it was called.

As Harry approached the bus interchange he saw a police car and two constables were standing out of the car talking to three youths, meanwhile on the opposite side of the road stood about seven youth's jeering at the police and hurling abuse at them, 'fucking useless copper cunt' and 'get a fucking life you fucking morons'.

Harry could see that the two constables were very nervous and he wondered why they had not called for backup and then he realised that it was just a waste of time as these two police just jumped into their car and drove off.

Harry knew that in his day, all seven of the abusive youths would be at the lockup sporting broken ribs and bruised kidneys and would be pissing blood for a week, but they would never, ever hurl abuse at a police officer again. How things have changed.

As Harry was about to get off the bus in the civic centre, one of the youths that had been verbally abusing the police back where he had got on the bus at the interchange, had been travelling on the same bus as Harry and was also getting off at the same stop, as he walked past Harry, just as the bus was starting to brake for the stop. Harry pushed out his right leg and the youth, aided by the inertia of the stopping bus, went flying down the aisle and collided with the handrail at the front of the bus. The youth, bleeding profusely from his nose looked back to see who had tripped him, just as Harry had walked past him with a snigger.

The next day, Friday and it was starting to rain quite heavily and it looked like any plans for the weekend were, in a nutshell, fucked. Harry didn't even notice the weather, he drove to work oblivious to the rain and his cars climate control automatically adjusted its interior temperature to twenty two degree's Celsius, he drove into his basement car park and walked into his office and was onto Google to try to find out what was in the basement next door to him.

He had simply typed in the address as sixty five Northbourne Avenue Canberra and added history and it came up as Jolimont and went on to say that in 1920 a timber building was erected at the site of 65 Northbourne Avenue on the Corner of Alinga Street and bounded by Moore and Rudd Streets, the building was originally constructed in England in 1899 for the use at Jolimont Railway Station in Melbourne and then later transported to Canberra in 1920 and was known as the Jolimont Building, in 1946 the ACT Police had vacated their station in Acton and moved to the Jolimont Centre and remained there until 1966 when they moved into a dedicated constructed complex in London Circuit.

'Well, said Harry to himself, 'I never knew that'. Harry then realised that what he had become lost in the other night in the dark, must be the old ACT Police station prison cells. It seemed, from what Harry was reading that the building suffered fire damage in 1969 and was demolished in 1977, the building that stands there now was constructed in 1981. And by the looks of it, thought Harry, it was built on top of the old police prison cells, wow.

Roger knocked on Harry's door, 'Harry, we have a fire rated partition that needs replacing in the old CBS building, do we have to get that certified?'

'You do Roger, but you also need to make sure that the contractor who constructs the fire rated partition has the appropriate license for fire rated construction and, he will also have to use a tested system for the required FRL'.

'Thought as much Harry, can you designate a system for that, it's 60/60/60 FRL',

'I'll do that for you old son, how soon do you need it?'

'No rush Harry, tomorrow's good, can you certify that also?'

'Yep, I certainly can Roger', Harry wanted to ask Roger a few questions to see if he knew anything about the basement next door. 'Are you a true local Roger?'

'I was born in O'Connor, lived here all my life, why do you ask Harry?', Harry had suddenly decided against asking Roger about the basement next door. 'Just wondered, no reason mate', Harry ended the conversation.

That afternoon, once everyone had gone for the day, Harry took his new rechargeable torch from the charger that was indicating a full charge, he also made sure his mobile phone was in his pocket and fully charged, this would give him a spare light if the same thing happened to the new torch and a way to contact help if he needed to do so. Harry headed off to the centre store room, he had placed the things that were in front of the door on his last visit, back as he had found them and now it all looked undisturbed, he unlocked the storeroom side doors and entered the corridor and followed it down to the steel door, then into the next corridor, he was amazed with the new light, it was an LED and it lit the whole place up. He found the reception room where he was when the light had failed on his last excursion then he found the toilet that he had fallen over with the old torch lying in the toilet pan. He pulled the old torch from the pan and noticed that there was no water in the bottom, he instinctively reached across and pushed the button to flush the pan, once flushed he could hear the cistern refilling, interesting Harry thought that the water was still on and with that thought in mind looked for a light switch, there was one near the doorway and Harry flicked it on, he could hear a light starter somewhere above him then suddenly the room he was standing in was brightly lit up, 'unbelievable' Harry thought to himself, 'why the fuck didn't I try that the other day'. Harry flicked off his torch and now moved around and found more light switches in different areas.

There was a long corridor with prison cell doors staggered on each side there were four doors on one side and three on the other, Harry tried a couple of them to find them to be unlocked. Harry then went completely through the whole complex, he was looking for another way into the basement, there must be one, he was thinking and then found another steel door at the end of the cell's corridor, it was unlocked and it led into a stairwell, Harry flicked his torch back on as there was no light in the stairwell and he couldn't see a switch. The metal stairs went up to about half of the ceiling height onto a small landing and then turned to the left, Harry walked up the stairs his foot sounds echoed and seemed to be quite loud, he slowed down and placed his feet down more gently to avoid making any noise and then saw the doorway at the top of the stairs. The doors opening direction was away from him, Harry slowly turned the cylindrical door knob and gently pushed it, the door did not move, Harry turned off his torch and looked at the bottom of the door, there was no light emitting from the other side. Strange thought Harry, the only way in and out of here seems to be by our storeroom door, that can't be right.

Harry had thoroughly searched the prison cell area, it was not a very large area and he did not think that it was the full size of the building above, he could find no other entrance, but he did find what may once have been a roller shutter in an open area and he assumed that it was once a small car park area and possibly a ramp up to street level. Harry needed a compass to work out exactly where he was and thought that he would bring one next time, he had tried the one on his phone but he could not get any reception. It seemed that no one had been down here for quite some time but he was sure that the main entry to the cells was by the doorway at the top of the stairs, maybe it was situated within an airlock, that would be the reason for the lack of light under the door.

Harry had returned to his office, placed his torch back on charge and placed the old torch into the garbage bin along with the charger. Harry had gone directly home this night as he and Val were meeting up with old friends, Don and Kathy Freeman, for dinner at the Hellenic Cross Club. Val was waiting for him as he arrived there to tell him that the dinner had been cancelled as Don had been involved in an accident in his car and was in the Woden Valley hospital. Val had told Harry that apparently, Don's car was tee boned at an intersection when a stolen car went through a red traffic light as it was being chased by a police car and into poor old Don, but, according to Kathy, he is alright, just shook up a bit but his car is a write off.

'Fucking kids, I'll bet' said Harry taking off his jacket then quickly replacing it, 'come on, we'll go anyway I'll call a taxi'.

The taxi arrived within twenty minutes and they headed off towards Woden to the club. It was very busy and it was just as well that Val had not cancelled the table that she had booked and she had told the maitre'd, with his enquiring looks, that their friends are running late. It was a bottle of 'La Adeline' rosé for starters while they decided what to eat. A grilled halloumi for two was enjoyed as an entree which finished off the rosé, next they both chose the rib fillet on the bone served medium rare and they selected a bottle of Louis Jadot pinot noir.

It had been an excellent evening and they even had enough of a win on the pokies to cover their costs of dinner and drinks, that wouldn't have happened if the Freeman's had been with them, as they don't play the pokies.

After waiting for about ten minutes in the freezing cold for a taxi, they decided to walk around to the taxi rank opposite the shopping mall on Corinna Street. Almost at the taxi rank when a car travelling towards them at high speed attempted to turn left into the Melrose Drive access, the speed that the car was travelling was much too fast to negotiate the turn resulting in total loss of control of the vehicle. The vehicle rolled a number of times coming into contact with Val and Harry Croft.

'Time to wake up Harry, come on Harry, wake up', a soft voice was calling him, but he didn't even remember going to bed. Harry slowly opened his eyes to Val's voice, but it was not Val's voice, the voice was coming from a young lady in a dark blue, casual type of uniform of a Canberra hospital nurse.

'Well, good morning Mr Croft, how are you feeling?', the nurse in the blue uniform was asking.

' I'm....alrig....where, what is happening" said Harry starting to sit up.

'No, stay down, you're fine', said the nurse re adjusting Harry's drip line and pushing the 'assist' button at the same time.

'You were involved in an accident Harry but you are doing fine' she said as a nursing sister came into the room.

'Good afternoon Harry, how are you feeling, you have been in a coma for a little while, please don't try to get up, the doctor is on his way to see you, please just relax', the sister soothed.

'How, how long have I,......where is Val,.. is Val here somewhere', Harry was becoming distressed, 'where is Val, please go and get Val'.

'The doctor won't be long now, please just stay calm and try not to move your left arm' was the sister's soothing response.

Harry lay still, his mind was trying to put things back

together, nothing was working, he was totally blank, it slowly started to come to him, the taxi rank and the speeding car, what happened, they saw the car start to turn and then it seemed to flip up in the air and then over and then......that was it, something must have gone wrong, his legs were hurting, he tried to move them, they moved but painful.

'Mr Croft,..' Said a voice with an Indian accent and Harry looked up to see a dark man wearing a pale blue top. 'My name is David Dharmani, how are you feeling Harry? you have been involved in an accident'.

'I'm not sure, but I want to know how my wife is', Harry was becoming very worried.

'I'm afraid your wife didn't make it, sadly she died early this morning I am sad to have to inform you'.

Harry did not hear any more words from the doctor or from the nurses, he was just in total shock, his thoughts were that maybe they made a mistake and it was someone else but not Val, no no no not Val, it can't be, why, but why why and how, it can't be right. He could feel the tears welling in his eyes, he could see her smiling and fussing about him as she always did, he always said 'what will I do without you' and now it's happened, can't be right, please let it be a mistake, he wanted Val to here with him.

It was three weeks until Harry could be released from hospital due to a hip fracture, his other minor bruises and lacerations had all cleared but it would be another three weeks yet until he could get around more normal and at three months until he would be totally normal. Harry was not looking forward to going home as the first thing he would see there would be signs of Val when she had left with him to catch a taxi to dinner, it was going to be painful and he knew it, but Harry had a much bigger challenge on his mind. Whilst in the hospital, Harry had many visitors and most made him feel very sad whenever they mentioned Val. Harry could not attend Val's funeral as he was confined to a bed but he watched it over and over on the television in his hospital room, first the live service and then the recording.

Amongst Harry's visitors was his boss Malcolm Tate, who told Harry that everything was fine and he still had his job just as soon as he was able. Other visitors were ACT Police officers, Detective John Simms and Detective Sergeant Barry Upfield to take a statement from Harry about what he could remember, which was not very much at all, Harry had thought about it for hours and hours while lying in his bed about what he did remember, what was the last thing he saw but it was all to no avail. The police filled in the blanks for him, one youth aged fourteen, and two youths aged sixteen, the fourteen and one of the sixteen year old's are brothers, were travelling in a BMW that was stolen from the suburb of Hughes about an hour before the accident, the vehicle travelling south on Corinna Street Phillip at approximately one hundred and forty kilometres per hour when the driver, the fourteen year old youth was driving the car, attempted to turn into the Melrose Drive connector and lost control of the vehicle. The three youths were unharmed in the accident and all three fled from the scene, video surveillance was viewed from three adjacent buildings to where the accident occurred resulting in positive identification of all three youths and they were all apprehended two days following the accident.

The youths appeared in the ACT Children's Court charged with Manslaughter, break and enter of premisses and theft of a motor vehicle, all were remanded on bail to appear for trial at a later date to be advised.

A shattered Harry had returned to his home and his job and tried to get on with life, his friends could not understand why he had not sold the house with memories and had really retired to somewhere away from Canberra, Harry's response was always 'soon, very soon'. Harry had maintained contact with Sergeant Barry Upfield as he had also been a friend of his late father Ted, (Tiger) Upfield who had been a colleague of Harry's back in his police days, but for a specific reason, Harry wanted to know when the youths would be attending court.

Things were good at work and it did not take Harry long to get his total mobility back, he had brought to his office on the day of his return, his old prismatic compass and his not so old DME, a laser measurement device. He again later that afternoon visited the adjoining building's basement but this time he did a rough sketch as he went from the storeroom door to the extent of the basement and terminated at the stairs leading up to level one of the building next door.

Returning to his office he went to his plan file cabinet and found the drawings for the Jolimont Centre that were kept as part of the ongoing maintenance for location descriptions. After two hours of transferring his rough sketch to drawing film, he could place it on top of the ground floor plan of the Jolimont Centre to form an underlay and locate precisely where the basement stairs rose to the ground floor of the building. According to Harry's calculations, the stairs would be near the Rudd Street end of the building next to a service duct. Harry looked closely at the drawing and made some notes about the service duct and took some measurements. The next day Harry contacted the Caretaker of the Jolimont Centre and made an appointment to meet with him as soon as practicable to inspect an item in the service duct at grid A section 4, the caretaker told Harry anytime, just drop in whenever it suits. Harry had gone to the Jolimont Centre at eleven o'clock that morning, taking the drawings with him for reference and also to make it look a bit official.

The caretaker was holding the end of Harry's tape and assisting Harry to make measurements near the service duct. The caretaker had the utmost respect for Harry since his first visit there when condensation was pooling on a section of tiled flooring and Harry had solved the problem within a matter of hours. Harry had found the entrance to the stairwell was closed in on all four sides by what seemed to be 200 series concrete masonry blocks which just did not make any sense to him, the caretaker told Harry that he had a full set of construction drawings in his office if he needed to check something.

'You're welcome to them Harry, I have never used them, I salvaged them from an old cabinet that was being thrown out'

'Thanks, that would be great if I could take them to my office and get them digitised then I will return them' Harry responded as he rolled up the full set of construction drawings for transit to his office.

Harry was pouring over the drawing in his office and checking each variation as it appeared and then discovered that the existing basement was to have been converted to subfloor parking but it was found that the entrance ramp encroached on the bounding property. It also showed a plan for the demolition of the existing cells and rooms but also showed a very expensive system of replacing these with structural columns and due to cost blowouts, it seems it was all scrapped and that the place was basically sealed off.

Armed with his new information, later that afternoon Harry again visited the basement but this time with some tools to enable the removal of some locks. The prison cell locks were Chubb custodial series mortice locks and Harry guessed that they would have all been 'keyed alike' so that only one key was required to be carried by the officer on duty to access the cells. The other three locks were Chubb vestibule locks that were on the interjoining steel doors and one set of 590 lock cylinders from the doors adjacent to the storeroom doors. These locks Harry took to a Locksmith located in the Fyshwick industrial suburb of Canberra. He instructed the Locksmith to recombinate the five cell locks and to key them alike, the vestibule and the 590 cylinders locks the same.

Harry had driven into the boarding town of Queanbeyan one evening to meet an old mate at Walshes pub, Nick Obodden was from Russia and had been working as a plastering contractor and a roof tilling contractor with his two brothers and four cousins in the ACT for as many years as Harry could remember. You really needed to be on the *right* side of these guys, Harry remembered as he walked into Walshes.

'Dobryy den Harry' shouted a heavy voice, 'your putting on the weight brother'

'Good day to you also' returned Harry, grabbing Nick's outstretched hand. Nick was a very athletic looking man at about fifty years old now, Harry guessed, but if you knew him well he was a good friend, you couldn't be his enemy because, as he had told Harry, 'all my enemies are dead'.

'You remember Bear'? Nick said as a giant of a man with the wildest unkempt dark reddish coloured beard walked up looking inquisitive.

'That's not that scrawny little prick that was your 'gofor' a few years back?' Then Harry started to realise that it was indeed one of Nick's very young cousins holding out his hand towards him.

'Gee Harry, you have changed a bit since I last saw you' said Bear, 'except you've got fatter, a lot fucking fatter actually', laughed Bear, c'mon over here it's my shout, and he ordered three schooners of VB.

'Vomit Bomb, be fucked' said Harry, 'get me a carton'.

The three of them sat at a table in the noisy bar and Nick came straight to the point and asked Harry what it was he wanted because the only time he ever comes to see him is when he wants something.

Magnus McCallum owned the Canberra real estate company known as Capital Real Estate and Auctions and was based in the suburb of Manuka.

'Certainly no lower than one point two million Harry, and I would imagine that it would sell fairly quickly, within two to three weeks, I would imagine' Magnus suggested as he walked through Harry's house.

'It won't be going on the market for that Magnus, try for another four hundred thousand and you can have the listing, I will still expect a contract on it within a month', Harry knew that this old Scott's prick wanted an easy sale for himself, 'and I'm not paying for advertising either you thieving old Haggis'.

Harry had approached Magnus at his office seeking a three month rental residential unit property, preferably furnished. He had also asked Magnus to appraise his home in Curtin and then form a marketing plan.

Magnus had found him a delightful, two bedroom unit on the third floor on Manuka Circuit in Kingston, just around the corner from the 'Kingo', one of Harry's old haunts. It was a fully furnished unit and had a lock up garage.

Harry had cleaned out his house and sold all his memories. His house was sold within three days for one point five million dollars, Harry said farewell to the old home that he and Val had shared for so many years and he tearfully turned his back on it, what a sad and cruel ending it had been thanks to the thoughtless and selfish actions of young irresponsible adults.

These 'young adults' as Harry had referred to himself, were they victims of society? They were brought up in an age where their parents did not believe in any form of punishment, and in fact, if these children were punished then the police could charge the parents for assault. The teachers in the schools that these children attended could not deliver any punishment against the students other than to send them from the class, otherwise, they also could be charged with assault. The police also had very little authority against the youth and were openly and publicly mimicked by these youths, if these people were arrested by the police there was always a good chance that charges would be brought about towards the police for abuse or false arrest by public defenders. The children could not be harmed, their parents would not get them inoculated for various diseases for fear it may harm them in some way or another, it wasn't the child's fault that they suffered from behavioural disorders. The parents would openly abuse the school teachers and accuse them of preventing their children from being responsible and educated young adults.

It was a great Saturday and a great drive out to Gunning to visit Val's sister Sonia and her husband Lex. Sonia was just a little older than Val and was a veterinarian and operated around the area, Lex her husband was more of an odd job man around the area, he had a tractor and slasher and a bobcat and other bits of machinery and did all sorts of work around the neighbouring properties.

Before moving to Gunning they had lived in the Canberra suburb of Duffy in quite an elite house on Eucumbene Drive, Sonia had a vet practice attached to the side of the house and Lex had a subcontract concrete truck that he drove. Lex was an American and a former US Navy seal and just loved fighting. Harry had pulled Lex out of the Canberra police lockup more times than he can remember and Lex was always indebted to him, as he said.

It was Lex's drinking and fighting that had caused them to move to Gunning and live on a property that was away from pubs as it was only a matter of time before Lex killed someone. On this day Harry had a beer with Lex and asked him if he could arrange a 10mm syringe and 100ml of xylazine and not to let Sonia know about it.

Lex told Harry that she left that sort of shit laying around everywhere and went to find some then and there, he was back within a minute with the syringe and a 500ml bottle of xylazine, saying that it seemed to be the smallest bottle of the shit that she keeps, Harry quickly placed it into his car then returned to finish his beer with Lex.

Sonia soon came out from whatever she had been doing in the house to join the boys in a beer.

'Seems you're busy inside there Sonia', Harry mused.

'Just getting three of the best looking rump steaks ready for dinner Harry and fixing the bed in the guest's room for you' said Sonia with a look of 'don't argue with me'.

Harry was expecting it and did not put up any resistance and merely went to his car and grabbed the carton of Great Northern stubbies that he knew that Sonia and Lex drink.

'You're a champ Harry', both Sonia and Lex said in unison, 'but you shouldn't have'.

Harry had replaced all the locks back into the cell doors and communicating steel doors in the basement of the building next door to his storeroom, he had also checked the plumbing in each of the cells to ensure that the toilet pans were flushing and that the wash basin taps were still tamper proof. The old watch house cells were in great condition considering their age, the locks on the doors worked exactly as they should and the acoustic barriers around the cell doors was remarkably intact, Harry had brought down a small radio and had turned it on to full volume and placed it into a cell, he had then close the cell door to find that the sound from the radio was barely audible, good.

The drive down the Clyde mountain was always quite enjoyable to Harry, but when you finally got to the bottom of it and past all the bends, you expected to be on the coast and it was quite a while until the Clyde river came into view and you were finally there, then through Batemans Bay onto Tomakin, a quiet little town on the beach that was once called Sunpatch with all the streets being named after Canberra suburbs. Colin Chrisp had been a fellow sergeant back in the day, although Col was a senior sergeant and quite often an acting inspector, but he did not want to be an inspector and failed every time they gave him the examination to become one. Col was a great mate and a great copper, his only down-fall was that he was always finding things that weren't yet lost, he was a procurer, if you wanted something then Col could most likely acquire it for you, but it was always the rule not to ask where it had come from. Even the top dogs at the station would ask Col if there might be a chance at getting a supply of the latest handcuffs that had just come out as their budget was blown out, Col would find a shipment of them and they would become ACT police issue.

Harry had 'self invited' himself to visit Col and his wife Helen, when he had called on the phone, Helen had answered and when he had hinted about coming down for a spell of fishing and maybe a few beers, Helen had said.

'For fucks sake Harry, you don't have to ask, just come on

down, you know where we are, we haven't moved, it will be good to get Col out of the fucking house for a bit, he needs motivation Harry, the sooner you get here and the longer you stay the better.'

'See you tomorrow, just after lunch' Harry had replied.

'Good, we'll all go to the sporties for lunch, I'd better wash my hair'.

They all enjoyed a great lunch at the club and a great 'get back together' then continued drinks at Col and Helen's place just down from the club. It was too rough and windy to take out their big boat onto the ocean the next morning so they all went in their smaller, 18ft boat on the river to do a bit of fishing and drinking and eating great oysters from the banks of the Tomaga River. And that night enjoyed a feed of flathead that they had caught in the river that day. Helen had gone to bed at around nine o'clock and Harry and Col had opened a bottle of port and had followed the tradition of 'throwing the top away', which of course mean't, to drink the whole bottle.

'What is it that you are after Harry'.

'What do you mean Col?'

'You know full well what I fucking mean Harry, don't be fucking stupid man, and whatever the fuck you are planning, I do not know and I do not want to know, but be fucking careful Harry, you are not a young man any longer and what-ever it is Harry, think about it and plan it properly. Now let's get out the chess board Harry'

They were on their third chess game and had reverted back

to beer as the port had diminished totally and out of the blue
Harry said.

'Nine millimetre Glock'.

'Ammo too?' Asked Col.

'Don't think that I would really need any ammo Col'.

'Harry, you know the old saying son, if you are prepared
to point it, be prepared to use it, a box of fifty'.

'Handcuffs?'

'I only have the old swing type, unless you can wait for a
couple of weeks. How many?'

'Four, should be enough, I don't mind the old swingers'
replied Harry with a giggle.

'No worries', confirmed Col, 'we can collect that tomorrow if you like, anything else?'

Harry could not believe this guy, he had a storage unit
in Moruya, which was about sixteen kilometres south of
Tomakin, we arrived there early the next morning and the
guy at the storage facility said hello boss to Col. After awhile
Harry had discovered that Col actually owned the storage
business, what a clever front if it ever got busted how would
Col know who the prick was that was storing illegal shit in
there. Harry wondered how many other storage lockers Col
had his special goods stored in.

Harry was now on a two week break from work and had
just arrived at Sydney's Mascot airport in preparation for his
flight with Qatar Airways to Palma. After the long, 29hour
flight and two stops combined it was good to get to the Hotel
Victoria Gran Meliá. Harry checked into his room and then
went down to the Terraza restaurant where he enjoyed a black

Angus rump steak and a bottle of Can Axartell pinot noir. Harry had an early night so he could be up early for the ferry trip to the Balearic Islands on the northeastern side of Palma. It was a seven hour trip to get there by ferry and he would be staying at the Hotel Catalonia Mirador des Port.

Another long day for Harry and he was relaxing at the bar with a cold beer wondering where to eat that evening. Harry was picked up at the hotel the next morning by the real estate agent who took him to see the house that Harry had found on the web in Cala en Bosch-Serpentona. It was about an hour's drive to the property and Harry just loved it from the moment that he had seen it on the internet. The agent had said the price was £470.000 and Harry offered £400.000 with an instant settlement.

The agent had made some telephone calls and returned to Harry and said 'Trato' meaning deal in Spanish.

'Going to have to learn this lingo' Harry nodded to the estate agent while shaking his hand on the deal, not bad he thought, seven hundred and sixty grand Australian dollars, still left him another seven hundred and fifty to buy a boat and stuff.

The estate agent then took Harry to the Banco Santander in Cittadella, the closest city to where Harry had just bought his house. Here Harry opened a bank account and transferred one point four million dollars into his new account and then transferred the deposit for the house to the estate agent with the balance to follow. The estate agent took Harry back to his hotel in Des Port where he insisted on buying dinner for Harry that night. The estate agents name was Marco, at about thirty years of age, Harry guessed, he looked pretty fit and was extremely polite, he also spoke very good English and told Harry that many British people now lived around Palma and that English was a popular language, so there was no rush for Harry to learn Spanish as most people now speak English.

Marco could not do enough for Harry and told him that when he moves over to live here, that he will meet Harry and help him to move in, not much to do anyway as the house he bought is furnished and he would organise the 'residence permit' the only thing that a foreigner requires to buy a house and live permanently in Spain.

Harry had returned to Canberra just in time for the Trial of the three youths who had been charged with manslaughter and theft. Barry Upfield had given Harry the 'heads up' on the court day although he had said to Harry that it was no good to him as it was a closed children's court and he would not get entry. Harry did not need entry to the court, Harry had only needed to know how many juveniles would be attending court that morning as it was a fair bet the the number attending would also be the same number leaving, as rarely were any juveniles held over in custody, it was always either a bond or suspended sentence.

Barry had told him that there would be five youths attending court that morning, the three charged with the manslaughter of Harry's wife and two others that were driving the stolen car that actually tee boned Harry's friend

Don Freeman, who was now a total paraplegic and living like a vegetable, and his wife, Kathy had recently suffered a heart attack due to the strain that had been recently placed on her as she tried to cope with her husband's condition.

Harry had contacted Nick just as soon as he had received the information from Barry and had told him, simply, 'five'.

Harry had listened to the news later that evening in his unit whilst eating a Pizza Hut pizza and drinking a Carlton drought stubbie. One of the boys convicted of manslaughter was placed on a two year good behaviour bond due to his young age. Another of the boys was given a five year prison sentence but wholly suspended on the youth being under parental care and the usual reporting to youth welfare officers due to his age of 17, the remaining boy who had previously offended was given a six year suspended sentence with similar conditions. They had killed an innocent person who just happened to have been there.

The other two boys who had been convicted of car theft both received two year good behaviour bonds. They had maimed an innocent man for life and had caused his wife to suffer a heart attack which she was unlikely to recover from.

What a fucking poor excuse of a justice system, it is not a justice system, these kids have no remorse, they have no respect nor feeling, and they could not care fucking less about what they have done, the lives they have destroyed, the hurt they have created and the pain, the pain that will never go away for so many people, but the courts don't give a fuck, the twenty year old psychologist who looked at and analysed the offences that these 'children' had committed had convinced the judge that they were unlikely to reoffend. How the fuck would she know and what dickhead of a judge would believe her, well fuck me, Harry thought.

Back at work and Harry had been very busy. Whilst he had been away much had happened and required a fair bit of input from Harry to get things into the 'outbox' and having done that he could now look at the other job he had at hand. Nick had sent Harry four addresses, in one of the addresses he had added the number '2', that would be the brothers thought Harry. Nick and four of his fellow 'bikie' mates had watched on the day of the court case for five youths exiting the court with their parents and then following them until they reached their respective homes and had recorded the addresses. Nick had guessed Harry's motive and had told him that the supply of each address was as far as they would go, no further, stated Nick.

Harry did not waste any time and started on the addresses one by one, his job gave him plenty of cover to be doing building inspections and or certifications so his absence was not going to be noticed. It was a simple thing to follow each youth in the morning to either their school or college, in either car or bus or walking as in the case of the younger brother of the two boys. Then the plan was to take each youth, one by one each afternoon in the same week which would take him exactly five days, just enough time to make it work, any longer could cause problems.

It was three ten on Monday afternoon when the first of the five was intercepted by Harry just as he had planned it, he had chosen the exit of an underpass and as the boy had walked out of the underpass, Harry, wearing a suit and displaying his old and out of date police badge, he stepped from his white Toyota Camry, just as the police were using, and called the boy over to him and then told him that he needed to speak with him at the police station, then simply opened the back door of the car. Harry had 5ml of xylazine loaded in the syringe that he held out of site in his hand that also displayed his badge and injected it into the youth's backside as he entered the car, he then followed by pushing the youth into the car and closing the door simultaneously, the startled scream would have been undetected and should any bystander have witnessed the whole operation, it would have looked like a normal police arrest taking place.

It was just too easy, Harry had in the back of his car the sixteen year old who had been with the brothers the night that Harry's wife had tragically died, he had gone out like a light and lay half and half on the back seat and the floor. Harry quickly slipped a pair of cuffs onto the youth with both his arms behind his back, just guessing with the xylazine dosage Harry estimated about thirty minutes before he may start to regain consciousness.

It was just on four pm when Harry drove down the ramp and through the roller shutter at his maintenance cell workshop and parked as close as he could get to the centre store room, he did a quick check to ensure that every one had left for the day the quickly dragged the youth from the car to the store room then through to the Jolimont basement doors which Harry had left purposely unlocked in order to get through quickly and then down the corridor to the first steel door.

It was at this point that Harry had realised that he had forgotten to bring the lock up keys with him, he had left them in the car. If he left the youth here on his own, he may regain consciousness in the short period that it would take Harry to go back to his car and retrieve the keys, he could not chance that, The steel doors also had a sliding bolt and a hasp to accommodate a padlock on the exterior side of the door and Harry quickly unlocked one handcuff and removed from the youths arm then placed it through the padlock hasp the quickly headed back to his car. As Harry exited the store room and headed towards his car he came to an abrupt halt, there was another car parked next to his in the basement car park.

'There you are Harry' said a cheerful Malcolm Tate, 'just dropped in to see how you were getting along with the back-log, looks like you are certainly putting the hours in old chap, are you coping OK?'

'Good to see you Mal', Harry said whilst trying to compose himself, and thinking fast, ' just came back to get my DME for an inspection tomorrow, I thought I would do it on my way in seeing that I live fairly close by to the site'.

'I just dropped off a memory stick for Veronica, I left it on her desk, it's a new monthly report format for head office', anyway I'd better keep going and let you get home Harry, see you later'.

'Yeah Mal, and thanks for your concern, keep in touch mate'.

Harry felt sick, he had messed up big time, and all his well laid out and time consumed plans had all just gone out of the door. He had never even considered the fact that someone could arrive here after hours and catch him out so easily. Harry knew that if he had not had the keys to the lock up in his car he may well have been caught in the act of imprisoning this youth. As it has turned out it is a good lesson learned, he will in the future lock all doors behind him so that if someone should arrive unannounced then they can't follow him into the lock-up, he would also acquire and install a small wireless camera somewhere in the basement car park tomorrow and connect it to his phone, that should solve those hiccups.

The youth was still slumped against the steel door, hanging with one arm from the hasp, Harry unlocked him from the hasp and then opened the steel door, dragged the youth through it then closed and locked the door behind him, 'no more surprises, Harry thought as he started to shake from the shock of almost getting caught then he turned on the corridor light.

What would he have done, he was thinking, he had been totally unprepared, caught out in total. He would have had to kill Malcolm, it would be the only way and then put his body in the lock-up somewhere, and then Harry realised that he didn't even have the Glock with him to shoot Malcolm with, had it got to that stage, 'must be getting past it old son, maybe nearly time to retire' he said to himself as he dragged the youth into the nearest cell that contained a bed, mattress, table, chair, stainless steel toilet bowl and wash basin. The youth had started to wake up and looked in sheer terror at Harry, he then started to become composed and looked around, in an arrogant voice he said 'What the fucks happening, where am I, is this prison?'

Harry, very calmly said to him while removing the handcuffs, 'Certainly is son, the judge had a rethink and gave you life', Harry laughed as he walked from the cell and then locking it said, 'Good luck'! The youth's screams and abuse were silenced as the door slammed shut. Harry removed the youths school bag from his car and went through it and removed anything relating to him then disposed of the bag in a hopper at the Manuka shops on his way home, exercise books were put through Harry's shredder at his unit and textbooks were dropped into Lake Burley Griffin, one down and four to go.

On reflection of what he had just done, and more to the fact to condone his own actions within himself, Harry knew that he had not physically harmed the boy in any way. He knew that by now the boy was becoming scared and that before very long, maybe five to seven days, the boy would become remorseful. These kids who are offending are aged anywhere between twelve and sixteen, so they were born around the just past 2000 mark. Physical punishment was banned in the ACT schools in 1988, NSW was 1990, SA in 1991 and Vic the earliest in 1985.

By 2006 all types of physical punishment was banned in both public and private schools. The prison population in Australia in 2012 was 29,400. In the year 2022 it had climbed to 40,600, the average age of prisoners is almost equal to the amount of years from 1988 to 2022 being 35.9 years of age.

Once the discipline in schools ceased, so did the respect from teenage children towards adults in general, meaning school teachers, police and parents. In the 1970s and '80s children referred to teachers as either sir or madam, miss or mrs, it is now a first-name basis or a nickname. Family members were called uncle or aunty, mothers were also known as mum, not by their Christian name, as with fathers. In today's society, a mother can be described as a 'birthing person' How gross is that?

In 1990 Australia ratified the United Nations 'Convention on the Rights of a Child'. In doing so the Australian Government agreed to prevent the harm or mistreatment of children, children are now defined in Australia as being under the age of 18. Sadly for Australia, the different states have different laws with respect to the discipline of children. Harry knew only too well what a ruler behind the knee, delivered by a Catholic Nun, felt like, as with six cuts on the fingertips of both hands from a flexible cane that was accurately wielded by a teacher in high school, or a leather strop that father kept for such occasions, not to mention the slap from mother either across the face or applied with great force on the calves of the legs. 'We had a deterrent in those days' thought Harry.

Harry had collected the other four youths in a similar method without too many minor obstacles, one was when two of the youth's friends had attempted to free him from Harry's custody and Harry had pretended to call for a backup with a paddy van, that seemed to scare them off. The situation now was that all five youths occupied all five cells in the old police lock up and it had taken five days to get them. It was by Wednesday that the media was reporting the disappearance of the first youth taken by Harry, his parents had simply thought that he may have just run away from home and blaming the repercussions from the trauma of appearing in court over a minor incident in the last week. Harry did not think that the death of his wife was a minor incident and remarks like this from the parents just demonstrated how incapable and irresponsible they were at being parents.

The youths had been left in the cells in the darkness with only water to drink from the basin. Harry had been taking loaves of bread down to the lock-up and had been placing two slices through the communicating hatch of the door, the sniffling and crying that he heard from each of them moved him emotionally and caused Harry to question himself on his quest for punishment but he convinced himself that no harm would befall the children, children that's a joke thought Harry, although, after three days in the cell, they were starting to sound like children, must be working thought Harry as they no longer seemed to have the attitude of 'you can't hurt me mister' and they had all actually stopped calling him a 'cunt' which Harry was pleased about as it was a word that disgusted him. He was pretty sure that they didn't know that the others were also in cells beside them. Harry had thought that it may seem worse to each as an individual to think that they were the only ones in the prison, rather than form a bond and gain strength through unity, it best he thought to keep them isolated.

On the following Monday following Harry's capture of the offending youth's, Harry had placed his formal resignation to the company's HR Manager Joshua Benthall, to take place in two weeks from the date of notice.

'Hello, ..Harry, it's Joshua here, the HR Manager'.

'Who, sorry...', joked Harry, he just could not help himself.

'Joshua, the HR manager' Joshua repeated,

'Ah yes, Josh, what is that I can do for you'.

'It's about your resignation Harry, just wondered why you might be leaving, maybe there is something more that the company could do for you, perhaps more money or a company car'.

'Josh, my dear Josh, if it were a case of more money you would be much too late, as an HR manager you need to keep in touch with your employees, not just when they tell you they are going to leave. It is your role to maintain communication with your people and develop a relationship with each and every one of them so that you will know if there exists any dissatisfaction in any form amongst them. Once they submit the resignation it is usually the end Josh and once you start losing too many of the good hands, then your position may be in danger' then Harry said farewell to Josh, 'yet another lesson for you to learn Josh, and don't forget that you do not stop learning until you are dead, Goodbye Joshua'. Harry hung up the telephone.

On the Thursday prior to Harry's last day with the company, Harry visited the boys in the cells, they were a wreck, each and every one of them seemed that they accepted the fact that they were here to die, Harry opened each access hatch on each door and said in a loud voice so that they could all hear him,

'Today is Thursday, you have been here for a mere two, to almost three weeks, it was only about forty years ago that men in Australia were placed in cells as these for the same crimes that you have committed and left in there for the term of their lives. I do not solely blame you for the crimes you have committed but rather the system, the society but more importantly, your parents. You will be set free in five days, consider yourselves lucky, when you leave here I know you will be different, tell your friends and your families what it had been like to have been here, if only for a short few weeks. I don't think any of you will want to come back and do it again. You may consider behaving like a human once you have been released. Harry then closed all the hatches just as the boys had started to shout out to each other and the room became silent again.

It was Harry's final Friday and luncheon was planned at the Marble and Grain restaurant on Mort Street, just a two block walk from the office. Harry had packed up last week and had vacated his unit, he had been living at the Meriton Suites for the last four days and was due to fly to Palma this evening. He had sold his car to a dealer and it was being collected from the basement car park at two pm that afternoon. At one thirty, following lunch Harry farewelled everyone and said he would send a postcard from the Gold Coast, he told Veronica that he would leave his keys on her desk at the office, together with his garage remote. Harry had also left an envelope on Veronica's desk that contained two Chubb keys and another standard key with a brief letter stating.

Veronica,

could you please contact the police and advise them that the five missing Canberra youths can be found in the old police cells of the Jolimont building.

These are the access and prison cell keys that they will need to release them. They were all in a very good condition when last seen on Thursday.

Kind Regards

Harry.

The police sergeant read Harry's note twice before he called for a backup at the Jolimont centre. He and the constable with him took the lift up to the ground level of the maintenance cell and walked to the main entrance of the Jolimont centre next door and they waited for backup. Detective Senior Sergeant Barry Upfield and his partner Detective Constable John Simms arrived as backup with another two uniformed police. Barry read Harry's letter and although he was confused he managed a grim grin, and then all six police officers went into the main entrance of the Jolimont centre. The caretaker was soon found and was told to lead the police to the basement to which he responded that there was no basement. Upfield told a uniformed constable to arrest the janitor and ordered a complete search of the ground floor to find the basement entrance, he then called for more backup.

With the search underway, the backup arrived and with it senior inspector David Prattman, Upfield handed Harry's note to Prattman.

'Where's the basement?' Prattman asked Upfield.

'Can't find it, the janitor said there is no basement', replied Barry Upfield. 'I've got him detained in the divvy outside'.

Prattman went outside to the police van to talk to the janitor and then told him he was free to go, Prattman then told Barry Upfield to check with the cell office where the letter had come from and ask them where the basement is, apparently, he said that the cell maintained the Jolimont centre so they should know.

'I've never heard of any basement other than this', said Veronica, 'but, let me check with the other guys' and she gave them all a buzz on the intercom and asked them all to come to her office as a matter of urgency as the police are waiting here. They all came around to Veronica's office and as soon as she mentioned the Jolimont basement, Roger said, 'I think that I might know where that is, but it's locked, or should be' and he escorted everyone out of Veronica's office and down to the storerooms area near the basement car park and he opened the centre store room with his key. They all walked in and Roger showed them directly to the double doors at the back and opened them both inward revealing the other set of double doors that opened outward, Roger tried the handle of the doors and demonstrated that they were locked.

Barry took the standard type of key from Harry's envelope and tried it in the door, he was able to unlock the double doors and then he pushed them both open revealing a very dark corridor, In fact, it was black, the only light was coming from the store room where they were all standing, 'Torch anyone' called Barry Upton and two of the four uniformed police came forward with torches from their tools belts. Barry took one of the torches and went through into the corridor and looked to his right where the corridor came to an end.

'This way' said John Simms as he was shining the other constable's torch to the left and down the corridor to another door that could just be seen. They all reached the door and Barry tried one of the Chubb keys in it and it worked, he unlocked the door and they fumbled in through the door, Barry called a halt and told the maintenance cell workers that they would no longer be required at this stage and that the police will want to talk to them later or tomorrow.

Barry shone his torch around but it was John who found the light switch and turned on the lights, they followed the corridor up to where it turned and discovered the the next steel door, the same Chubb key also opened this door and they all passed into the anteroom with the large window looking down another corridor with two cell doors to one side and three cell doors to the other. Barry walked up to the first cell door and tried the same Chubb key, it would not enter the lock, the other Chubb key unlocked the cell and a scream was heard within the dark cell. The light switch adjacent to the cell door was soon found and turned on revealing a youth just standing there looking confused, he mumbled something about how he had been waiting for them and then started crying uncontrollably and asking for his mother. They then unlocked the remaining cell doors to find the five boys all safe but very shaken up and none were feeling well, ambulances were called and the cars parked in the basement car park were moved to make way for them. Amazingly all five youths that had been missing for nearly three weeks had been found alive.

Harry had been shown by one of his neighbours how to brew and keg beer at his new home, his other neighbour wanted to show him how to make wine but Harry decided that beer would be enough for him, although he did admit that the neighbours wine had a very good taste, a very nice burgundy he thought.

Harry had now been back on the island for three months and had heard very little from Australia, the bits of news that he did get did not mention much about the ACT. Harry did not have internet on the island as he did not want to become addicted to it as many people his age tend to do and, anyway who gives a shit about the ACT. He knew he was safe here from the police as Spain has no extradition treaty with Australia, that's why he chose Spain, sure he got homesick and missed watching the NRL but there was plenty to do here, or nothing if thats the way it suits you. Harry's house had a great pool with a huge outside living area and it was a big home with four bedrooms and three bathrooms, much too big for just him but he knew the kids would come for a visit one day.

He had just finished kegging a brew of beer into three nineteen litre kegs and was enjoying his third schooner when a voice called out to him. The home was very secure with a high fence that surrounded the entire property and had a secure double steel bar gate that was securely fixed to the high stone wall, the garage door was always closed and locked,

'Harry, are you here?.....Harry'

'Who is it?' Asked Harry

'Me, Nick, Nick Obodden....'

'Fuck me' called out Harry with glee in his voice, 'you are fucking kidding me mate, what the fuck are you doing here'.

'Long story Harry, but let's have a beer first mate' Nick said looking through the fence at Harry's half finished schooner on the table. Harry went and got his key to let Nick in, he was so happy to see a friend from Australia, it had only been three months but it did seem much longer, Harry grabbed a cold schooner glass from the outdoor fridge beside the kegerator and poured Nick a coldie.

'Cheers Harry', Nick said as the beer glass went to his lips, 'my god, that is good, very good Harry'.

Nick had parked his somewhat large bag on the ground next to the outdoor table and now sat down on a chair next to the table and Harry.

'What a surprise Nick, gee it is good to see you mate, are you going to stay for a bit?' Harry asked, hoping that he was going to stay.

'Mate, if you don't mind and can handle some bad company, then I'd love to stay for a while, like a month or so if that's ok?'.

'As long as you want to mate........'.

'I'll pay my way' interjected Nick, 'I'm not here to bludge on you Harry'.

'I couldn't give a fuck if you did mate, but, tell me....why are you here?' Harry asked Nick.

'The same reason you are here mate', grinned Nick.

'I do not want to know', so what's all the news', said Harry taking Nicks and his glass to refill them.

'That's a nice drop of beer Harry'.

'It's home brew, believe it or not, the bloke next door, whose name I can't pronounce, showed me how to make it and got me started'. Harry went on to tell Nick about the other neighbour who made a good wine, he told him about the good fishing, the cheap, but excellent beef that was available and the general run of the place and he once again told

Nick how happy he was to see him and that he could stay as long as he wanted.

Nick did tell Harry it concerned him that he was so easy to find here, in fact, Nick had said, it seemed that everyone knew the new 'Guiri' in town and I had no worries getting directions. Harry said that he wasn't really in hiding as he knew the Australian coppers could not touch him out here, and besides, Harry slipped the Glock out from his pocket and back in. Nick thought that was a good idea and that he was now glad that he had called out.

Harry and Nick had a great time around the island and Nick was most impressed with the quality of the food, he had thought that it might have been a bit warmer but at least it was not cold, Harry had reminded him that it was winter. They had both bought a Vespa moto (scooter) each and Harry could not believe that he had not done that earlier, so much easier than dragging the Jeep out when he needed something from town.

Nick had now been on the island with Harry for about five months and they really got along well, more like a father and son relationship which seemed to work well. Harry was pleased that Nick had turned up out of the blue, he needed someone to talk to at least, but this was good, they took it in turns cooking and even brewing the beer, which could not have been better. Harry had thought that if Nick had have called him first before coming to the island, then he thought he would most likely have told him not to come as he would not be welcome, strange, he thought, how things just turn out.

Harry had returned from the town with some beer brew extract and rump steaks. He parked his moto next to Nick's out the front of the entrance to the house and he went inside carrying the bag he used to transport his things on the moto to find Nick inside the house standing in the main reception room with the two detectives that Harry knew from Canberra. Harry's hand instinctively went from the bag that he was carrying to his right side pocket, then to the sudden call from Nick..

'Woha... wo.. wo Harry' Nick called out urgently to Harry, 'It's ok,...it's ok' he said as he moved towards the two detectives and held up their arms to show Harry that they were both locked together with handcuffs.

'What the fuck is going on here' asked Harry, whilst trying to maintain his rage and placing his bag down to the floor, 'are these blokes here for you Nick?', Harry was pretty wild and getting a bit wilder.

'No, no...Harry just settle for a minute', Barry Upton started to plea, 'just listen for a moment.......'

'Just shut up copper cunt, I'll do the talking', said Nick as he pushed both of the detectives to the ground.

Nick went on to tell Harry to relax and get a drink for both of them and he will explain what he knows and not to listen to the lying pricks of coppers. Harry restored his cool and went and came back with drinks. Harry told Nick that he was hoping that what he was going to say would be good. Nick had replied that it was pretty fucking unbelievable. Nick had been in the pool when Harry had gone into town, and after about twenty minutes Nick had heard a noise coming from inside the house and had just assumed that it was Harry back from town, so he stayed in the pool just floating on his back, then he heard the back door open and close, and then open and close in quick succession which made Nick cautious and he let himself sink to the bottom of the pool, he then came up slowly and peeked over the edge of the pool to see the two goons sneaking past the pool to the garage, side by side peeking in the garage window. Nick had then, as he said, simply leapt from the pool and grabbed a head in each hand at each side and just slammed them together and they just fell in a heap, the useless pricks he added. Nick had then found that one of them was carrying cuffs so he cuffed them together,

Barry Upton was looking at Harry and he looked like he did not know what to say.

'I really hope Barry, that you can tell me why you are here, it needs to be good Barry or this is not going to end well' Harry said.

'I can explain, I really can, and we only came here to basically say hello, it's true Harry, as silly as it sounds Harry it's true. Barry said pleadingly. He went on to tell Harry that Canberra had issued a warrant for his arrest and as we had no treaty with Spain, it was decided by the hierarchy that we should just simply come over here and persuade you to come back with us on your own free will so you can explain to the Canberra judges what you thought you were doing by kidnapping juveniles.

'We knew it was never going to work Harry', said John Simms, 'we just came for the holiday and to look you up to tell you that you are a hero in Canberra, to us and the public'.

Simms continued to explain to Harry that when the kids were released by the police and had made statements, the media got hold of the story, it was leaked actually, Barry Upton had added, and it seemed to have a huge impact on the youth crime in the ACT.

Some Canberra residents were so motivated by the story of a bit of justice that was finally happening to the 'untouchable' youths in Canberra that they formed vigilante groups and started to round up any kids they could find around the suburbs or shopping centres and even pubs, they would then take these kids on a drive down to the cotter and strip them naked and remove their shoes, throw buckets of cold water over them and then leave them to walk back to town.

Some vigilantes, sadly went way too far and actually inflicted injuries to some of the kids and in one incident the kid died. But it had a great impact Harry, juvenile crime almost ceased within a week, stolen cars dropped from around three hundred a week to about five, it was just brilliant what you have started Harry. But the law is the law Harry and some dickhead politician decided that we had to get you back to pay for your crime, fuck knows why, but anyway, we volunteered to come over to ask you to return with us.

'We knew, Harry, that from the start it was a dumbfuck, political idea, and it had no chance of working, but we thought, well,...hey, let's do it and say hello to Harry, enjoy a holiday and then tell the dumb pricks back in Canberra that we couldn't find you' Barry Upton concluded'.

'Is that really the truth Barry?' Asked Harry pulling his Glock from his pocket and aiming it at Barry's head.

'No No.....no Harry' said Nick, 'there is a much better way' and taking the Glock from Harry he asked him if he had just happened to get this gun from Crispy, Colin Crisp? Harry looked at Nick quizzically then replied that he had, yes but why?

Nick did not answer Harry but removed the ammunition magazine from the grip of the Glock and then went up to Barry Upton and forced his, uncuffed hand, around the Glock, he then returned with the Glock to the table and reinserted the magazine, then placed the Glock on the table. Nick then looked at Harry's copy of the local directory and made a phone call on his mobile.

'Sí, necesitamos a la policía en Cala en Bosch-Serpentona 46, intento de secuestro' spoke Nick in very good Spanish, he then ended the call and calmly told Harry that he police are on their way to an attempted abduction at this address. We have thwarted their attempt by overpowering them and disarming them of their ACT police issue Glock and have secured them with their ACT issue handcuffs. I think Harry, that these two super sleuths may be in the shit and I think that it will be a long time until they are returned home to their families.

'Fucking brilliant mate, just fucking brilliant' Harry exclaimed.

'You've got it all wrong Harry' called Barry Upton.

'Good luck Barry and you too John, you fucking pair of arseholes' replied Harry. 'Remember when the Federal Police tried to do the same with Skassie? I think those cops are still in Madrid somewhere'.

The Spanish police were there within seven minutes and

quickly took in the scene, they took possession of the Australian issued police gun and exchanged the Australian issued police handcuffs for those of Spanish issue and marked these items as evidence, they arrested the two trespassing Australian police officers and asked Harry and Nick if they could please come to the police station tomorrow, at any time that may be convenient, to make statements. Harry and Nick assured the police that they would be at the police station in the morning and bid them goodnight.

Both Harry and Nick were struggling to contain their laughter throughout the ordeal and now, both were almost uncontrollable.

'You are a fucking legend Nick' said Harry in between laughs, 'I am so glad that you came to visit and forgot to go home'

"Mate, I was thinking the other day how vulnerable you are here and then I thought of Skase and remembered that he got abducted by the Fed's but it all went wrong. But, just looking at this scenario, I reckon there is a way we can we make you become reincarnated' Nick was saying as his mind was going into overdrive.

Harry stopped laughing and looked deadly serious at Nick.

Nick said to Harry that, 'Those pair most likely won't be the last, and they may even be more vengeful now these pair have got nicked, haha, nicked, pardon the pun, he then asked Harry what was his plan, did he want to return to Australia?'.

'Yes Nick, I would like to go back to Oz, this place is great, don't get me wrong, but I do miss Australia'.

The next morning they both fronted up at the 'Guardia

Urbana' and each made a statement which took absolutely ages to do, they had both assumed an hour or two at the absolute most but it had to be written in Spanish and the guy typing the statements was not too good at English.

The 'Guardia' had already established that Upton and Simms were working for the Australian Federal Police and that, officially, they were both on annual leave. The Glock had been identified as the property of the Australian Federal Police - ACT Policing Division and had been reported as stolen some years ago. The handcuffs were also identified as AFP and in current issue to a Senior Constable Robert Sharp. It was a common occurrence that cuffs got moved around between officers during the course of arresting suspects and adding additional cuffs to transfer them.

Upton and Simms had already appeared in court that morning and had been remanded in custody to face trial on a date to be announced, the local Official de Policia, told Harry and Nick that their case would not come up until about the middle of next year as there was a huge backload on the courts. More sniggers from Harry and Nick and they were free to go and 'muchas gracias'.

'What would you say Harry' Nick said in between drinks of his beer, 'if I told you that Skassie is actually in his mid seventies and is living in Australia?'.

'Well', replied Harry, also sipping a beer, 'I would say, no more beers for you old son'.

'If you don't ask too many questions, I will tell you what we did for Skassie and I reckon it would also work for you'.

'Who is 'we' and what the fuck are you talking about'.

'Too many questions already Harry' laughed Nick and told Harry what he had mean't and how it was done and could be done again. Harry told Nick that it all sounded pretty good to him but he would wait until the morning to have a think about it.

Harry was already in the pool at seven thirty the next morning when Nick came out to cook breakfast, Harry climbed out of the pool and wrapped a towel around him and said to Nick,

'Sound's good to me, let's do it'.

'We have not yet discussed the fine details Harry and it won't be cheap, nobody is going to help us for nothing you know'.

'What sort of a cut would you want Nick?'.

'I have thought about that Harry and what I want for my 'cut' as you call it, is your house here on the Island..'.

'Fuck off........'.

'At least wait till I'm finished,......Your house, this house, for the price that you paid for it, I think you mentioned around the $750.000 mark? It would be at least a million Australian dollars on today's market, and....besides, aren't we good mates?'.

'You are a good mate, Nick, you really are. Thanks mate'.

The first thing that Harry got onto was a new identity and the only person he knew was Crispy. When he told Colin Crisp what he was going to do, Col took over the conversation, 'Let me see, passport, driver's license, medicare card, credit card and a tax file number, I can only do an ACT drivers licence, so if you go to another state you will have to change it, same as your bank account, but that is a piece of piss to transfer, both are really. Now roughly that will cost you....around the sixty grand mark all up and that will include ten grand in your new bank account'.

'Fucking do it Crispy, go for it you champ', was Harry's response.

The sale of Harry's house was just so unbelievably simple thanks to Marko, the real estate agent who had sold Harry his house when he first came to Spain, he had simply organised everything so swiftly including the permit for Nick. Nick had paid Harry in part Australian and part Spanish cash for the value of the house as he knew that was what Harry needed the most just now. Harry had told Nick that if he could not handle that amount of dollars for the house then they could sort it out later. Nick had told Harry not to ask questions but thanks for his concern towards his financial position, but the truth was that if Harry needed a couple of million dollars in a hurry, then Nick could accommodate him. Harry was impressed.

It wasn't hard to find an undertaker who knew of a man that would be dead within a month due to a failing heart and it had been diagnosed that the next heart attack, would sadly be his last, this man was told not to drink any alcohol of any description and the undertaker could organise a bottle of grappa for him at any time. His family could not care if the funeral for their esteemed grandfather included a body in the coffin or not for €1000,00 and the same for the undertaker to deliver the body to Harry's house, that price would also include shaving all the hair of the corpses head and to dress into Harry's clothes to make it slightly resemble Harry.

It was deemed by Nick to be just too risky to try to bribe the local doctor for a death certificate but that any doctor that had never met Harry would really do.

Next was Harry's will, it wasn't very difficult as he was leaving everything to Nick, which included the house and the contents plus the balance of Harry's bank account, a very simple matter done at the local village with the local solicitor.

Once Harry had a new name and identification then he would set up a bank account at the same bank where he presently had an account. Nick would also set up an account with the same bank, that way, Harry's 'will' money would be an internal bank transfer to Nick. Once Harry's new account was established Nick would simply transfer to that account a fixed amount on a weekly basis that would result in Harry's account balance being equal to that of his total will value. Harry would also organise a weekly rent payment to Nick's account just to add a little confusion. Very simple and the weekly transactions within both accounts are unlikely to be noticeable as it was an internal bank transfer.

So it was all set, a new ID was being set up for Harry with a passport showing an arrival in Spain, for this Harry had to send his legitimate passport to Colin Crisp in order for him to transfer his page with his arrival stamp for Spain to his new ID. Harry was dying to find out what his new name might be, but Crispy had told him that 'dying' was actually the crux of the matter as he needed someone to die that was around Harry's age and, fairly soon!

The undertaker had contacted Nick and had asked what day did he want the body? as to get the body, still warm, as it were, he would need to know what day so he could organise a drink for the victim. Nick had asked the undertaker to wait on the phone for a moment and called out to Harry and told him that tomorrow he would die, OK? He then told the undertaker to go for it and he would have the cash ready for him when he arrived tomorrow afternoon with the body. Done.

It was the worst day that Harry could ever remember, Nick told Harry to relax, he wasn't really going to die, someone else was doing it for him, and this made Harry worse. The undertaker had arrived at three o'clock that afternoon with the body and had proceeded to shave the face and the head of the body. The undertaker had gone to the man's house at nine o clock that morning with a bottle of very bad grappa, the man had enjoyed the grappa and had thanked the undertaker, his old friend from school days, for the excellent grappa. He had drunk half of the bottle and suffered a major heart attack, as advised that he most likely would if he drank alcohol by his doctor, who was called instantly and consequently issued his death certificate on the spot to allow the undertaker to remove the body and prepare it for burial.

Now the dead man was shaved and dressed in Harry's favourite floral shirt and his best Colorado shorts and was lying next to Harry's outdoor fridge where he kept his home brew beer. First, the ambulancia was called and attended within a remarkably short time, they attached an oxygen mask to the body and tried resuscitation but without any favourable result, it seemed that Harry had suffered a massive heart attack and was unconscious. The ambulancia had taken Harry to the hospital where he was pronounced dead on arrival. Poor Harry.

Meanwhile Nick had closed all the window shutters at Harry's, now his house, as a mark of respect for the passing of his old mate Harry. This also assisted in the real Harry to move around the house without being seen by any inquisitive eyes. Harry would have to remain in hiding for at least two months, Nick had estimated. He had also suggested that he grow a beard and wear a hat, a thing that Harry never did, and just remain quiet and calm. Harry had told Nick that it seemed to be easy for him to say,

'You're not the one that's dead' said Harry and burst out laughing and so did Nick.

'This is going to work Harry, no worries'.

Harry's death certificate was issued by some intern at the hospital and Harry's funeral took place three days later, not allowing time for any relatives or friends to attend from Australia. The only people at the funeral was Nick and the undertaker, who was now well known by the late Harry.

Nick had the undertaker contact the Australian Central News Agency for an obituary insertion which was quickly picked up by AFP and Harry's son, Scott who had alerted Harry's friends of his sad passing, some of which were members of the AFP. This really hurt Harry, that his son would think that his father was dead, but as Nick had said, no one could fake being sad at a funeral and the cops would be watching his son Scott and Scott's wife Zoe, like a hawk. It just had to be.

About seven weeks after the funeral, Nick had received a package in the mail from Fernandalio Cruzimorsz from Melo in Uruguay, it contained Harry's new identity with a letter from Colin Crisp. The letter contained very strict advice from Colin, Nick read out the letter;

It is imperative that this letter is destroyed once you have read it.

You will find in this package (1) a current Australian passport in the name of Dennis Harold Sutton, male, born in Victoria Australia 1959, the person described on the passport and photograph are of Harry Croft, the passport also showed an entry into Spain two weeks prior. (2) State of Victoria Drivers Licence, complete with date of birth and photograph of Harry Croft. (3) NAB Visa card issued to Dennis Sutton with an attached saving bank account, the balance on the Visa is $20,000 available credit, the balance on the savings account is $10,000.(4) Australian Tax File Number.

It is important that you do not enter any Australian Casino's or rail transit centres as these establishments will most likely have a photographic facial recognition description of Harry Croft and the AFP will be immediately alerted if any of these devices are triggered by a photographic scan of you. These devices recognise facial features and the growth of a beard will not prevent identification, so unless you want to undergo cosmetic or plastic surgery, stay away from any type of these devices.

Residential address should not be popular tourist areas where there may be a chance of someone holidaying from the ACT who may recognise you, well populated cities should also be avoided due to the widespread use of facial recognition camera's. Nor are small towns advisable due to the close knit of these people who seem to take delight in finding out exactly who the 'newcomer' may be and also a bored local police officer.

Rather a regional centre with a population of around 60,000 to 100,000 would be a better and safer place to live anywhere in Australia, or overseas for that matter.

Good luck Harry, or Dennis, whichever you chose.

'That man is nothing short of a genius Harry,...I..mean..Dennis' said Nick with a grin.

'It's all done, just like that, unreal...just..unreal, I mean like,..how on earth', responded Harry. 'But I think I will stick with Harold, Harry, yes,...Harry Sutton, I can get used to that'.

Harry was quite intrigued with the way that Nick had organised his change of identity and quizzed him on his knowledge of how such things can be done. Nick had told Harry, in confidence, that he was the one who had planned the escape for Skassie. Nick had worked for him in Port Douglas as his personal bodyguard after Skassie had bailed him on manslaughter charges and then had supplied Queensland's top barrister to defend Nick.

Nick had left Australia with Skassie and is wife and had come to Santa Ponsa at Majorca where they had bought a villa. It had been Nick's idea to create a new identity for Skassie after a few failed attempts to abduct him and return him to Australia, so he had done basically the same thing that he had just done for Harry, with the exception that Skassie had paid Nick five million dollars for his efforts,. Skassie had remained in Spain for seven years following his fake death and then moved back to Melbourne in Australia where everyone had forgotten about him, Nick assumed he was still living there as at 2022.

'Five million from Skassie, yet you want nothing from me?' Harry said feeling a bit confused.

'Skassie was a fucking thief mate, he was a criminal, you are not, you helped solve a big problem with juvenile crimes in the ACT, it's something the coppers there should have done and long time ago but were too gutless to even try. They let those punks run circles around them, they are embarrassed Harry of what you have done and they didn't even try, they just followed the book, 'you can't strike the youths as you will be put on report and it will be *you* that gets a kick in the arse' and that was their way of thinking. You are a hero mate, what Upton was saying about that would be true and they are all fucking jealous'.

Harry had been growing a beard for the last six weeks and had made this go permanently grey by the use of bleach when showering, he had shaved his head of hair and he had also lost about twenty kilograms in weight and now looked remarkably different. He had decided to test his new looks on the neighbour who had shown him how to brew beer.

He had knocked at the neighbour's door and when the neighbour had opened the door, he had not shown the slightest recognition, he had said to the man that he was looking for his late cousin, Harry Croft's former home and the neighbour directed him to the house next door and told him to ask for Nick.

Harry was now convinced that he had taken on a new

identity that had certainly worked with the neighbour whom he had known fairly well since his arrival in Spain, he now felt confident to return to Australia, all he had to do was plan where to go to make a new start with his new name. But there was no rush now he had altered his appearance and he could easily get by as Harry's cousin, who was also called Harry. Well, it happens!

Harry was in deep thought about returning to Australia, it was now almost ten months since his new ID and the demise of the old Harry, he was homesick, true, but for what? He no longer had a home in Australia, he no longer had a wife, and he couldn't look up any of his old mates. His only real connection with Australia was his son Scott and his wife Zoe and of course his grandson who was about nine by now Harry guessed.

One afternoon while sitting and enjoying beers with Nick, Harry had decided to ask Nick for some advice.

'Nick, my old son, you....being the man of the world, which you surely are,......how would you suggest I go about contacting my boy Scott?'.

'I was actually wondering when you would come around to this, you have lasted longer than I thought you would, it's not that hard to do Harry but it must be done carefully, you don't want to blow all the hard work that has been done on your new ID. One wrong move mate and it's all been for nothing', Nick then also reminded Harry that , 'as he should know quite well, the cops would still be watching Scott like a hawk. Also remember Harry, that you have been out of the force for over twenty five years, that my friend is a fucking long time and lots of things have fucking changed. For instance, as an example,.....if you called Scott on his mobile, the cops would instantly know that a call from this area we are in now was received by Scott, they may even have a warrant to record all his telephone conversations and the same could also be true for Zoe'.

'So you are saying that it is out of the question'

'I didn't say that! Harry, no,...it's not out of the question, but it's still risky,.....what we do is get Scott to call you'.

Nick told Harry that the first thing they would do tomorrow was to organise Scott to call him, 'You'll see'.

The next morning they went into Cittadella on their moto's and went into the Telefónica store and bought two Galaxy A24 mobile telephone's complete with a sim card and international roaming. They then placed the number of each phone into the relevant contact section of each phone, in order for each phone to be able to contact the other. They then went to the Cittadella Correos (post office) and bought three different sized padded envelopes. Nick then asked Harry to write Scott's address onto a padded postage envelope that was just big enough to accept one of the Galaxy telephones. Nick then wrote a name and Canberra address onto a larger padded envelope and placed Harry's envelope inside this, he then took yet another larger padded envelope and addressed it to a person in New Zealand and placed the second padded envelope, which contained Harry's padded envelope inside it, he then went to the desk and paid for the postage to New Zealand and dropped the package in to the mail receiving bin.

'You now wait for a call from Scott', said Nick, 'Scott

will recognise your hand writing on the envelope that he will finally receive, well should recognise your writing, I suppose, then he will see the number stored on the phone and hopefully will call it"'.

'Sound's like a lot of 'ifs' said Harry, but he was quite impressed with the way Nick had set that up so simply and quickly, this man was definitely the man to keep on the right side of him. As it had been said about Nick previously, 'He had no enemies, they were all dead', Harry could well believe that.

It was just over two weeks that they had sent the telephone to Scott that the other Galaxy telephone had rung. It was eleven fifty on a Thursday night that the Galaxy had started to ring, fortunately Harry was just on his way to his bedroom when he heard the telephone's distinct tone that they had set, he raced down stairs and just missed the call. He had immediately called the number back but it gave the busy signal, as he was trying to call the number again the telephone rang , it was Scott.

'Is that you dad,....really......really' called Scott, his voice starting to stutter.

'Mate, I know I have a lot of explaining to do, I understand that it must be a great shock'

'Oh dad, I can't believe it, it's unreal'.

After a lengthy conversation, during which Scott admitted that he had strongly suspected that Harry, his father was not in fact dead, and a friend of his at his work, who happened to know one of Nick's sons, had told him not to be surprised if he discovered his father was still alive. They had lots to talk about as it had now been just over a year since Val had died, it seemed that in no time Harry's phone was giving a low battery warning and Scott had replied that his was also, they quickly made another time and day to make contact again.

During the many conversations that Harry had with Scott and also Zoe and young Morgan, the possibility of an actual meeting was discussed in great length only to decide that the risk was just too great. During one conversation with Zoe, she mentioned that things were not too good with Morgan and that they had discovered that the local priest had interfered with him whilst he had been at alter boy practice. She had told Harry that Scott had not wanted Harry to know as he he knew just how wild that you would get if you found out and that there is nothing now that can be done as the priest has now been moved along to another Parish.

'Zoe, listen to me', Harry was instantly at boiling point, 'what do you mean there is nothing that can be done, how is Morgan reacting to all of this'

'He refuses to go to church and he didn't want to go back to his private school, we have enrolled him into the local public primary school and he is just starting to settle down and get back into school interests,...hang on Harry, Scott wants to talk to you.....'

'Dad, don't worry, everything has been taken care of, everything is fine now, the priest has gone and.......'

'Bullshit everything is fine Scott, fucking bullshit Scott, who is this mongrel, what the pricks name.....'

'Dad, please, let it go'.

'You know I won't' and Harry finished the call, he was

ropable, it was almost midnight when he went outside to pull a schooner of his brew, he was still there when Nick found him at about eight o clock the next morning, just brooding.

Harry told Nick about the priest and his grandson, Nick shook his head in disbelief.

'What would you do Nick?'

'Harry, if it was me, and I am glad it's not, but if it was, then I would go over and put the pricks lights out'.

'I reckon that's what I might do Nick, I'll have to work out a bit of a plan'.

'NO, HARRY.....WE'LL work out a plan, a good plan'.

Nick had suggested to Harry, for starters, piss off that useless iPad and go and buy a decent laptop computer, get a MacBook Air and get the top of the range, make sure it has the M2 chip in it. Nick had already upgraded the internet connection at the house with Balear WiMax and with that combined to Harry's MacBook he shouldn't have any problems doing his research.

Harry's first task, set by Nick, was to find out the priests full name and a bit of background, he told Harry that the catholic church are very talented when it came to hiding priests as they have had so much experience at it.

Harry had started on Facebook for any social pages on the priests former church, so simple to make up a false name and email address on Facebook. Harry had used the name of Denise Potter for his account together with a 'G' mail address. He had to go on line at night as Palma was nine hours behind Australian time, he had found a Woden Valley Church group and had placed a request to join the group and while waiting to be accepted read whatever he could on the Vatican and it's comments and views on pedophile priests and could not believe the reports that are available through Google.

One report estimates that 216,000 children were abused by priests between 1950 and 2020, and that accounting for abuse by other church employees increases the total number to around 330,000. Around 80% of the victims were boys.

Harry found that there were virtually hundreds of documents on the web in respect to priests., but there did not seem to be very many clues on how to bring it all to an end

Another question on Google was;

How many priests have been accused in Australia?

Between 1950 and 2010, more than 1,200 Catholic clergy in Australia were the subject of child abuse allegations. As an indication of the extent of the abuse, the Commission calculated that, over the same 60-year period, seven percent of all the country's Catholic priests were alleged perpetrators of child sexual abuse.

And on May 9, 2019, Pope Francis issued the Motu Proprio Vos estis lux mundi requiring both clerics and religious brothers and sisters, including Bishops, throughout the world to report sex abuse cases and sex abuse cover-ups by their superiors.

Well, thought Harry, 'That will work'.

Harry's request to join the Woden Valley Church group was accepted and he was permitted access to their page, he immediately began to scan the page and went back into the pages history and actually found a section welcoming the new priest to the group;

From the group committee, we extend a warm welcome to Father Jeremy Ironside, formally from Bendigo Victoria.

That was all Harry wanted, armed with the priests name and a landline phone number for the church, both Harry and Nick approached one of Nicks friends, a very pretty Spanish lady, Carmen, who spoke quite remarkable English.

Timing it correctly to around eleven o clock in the morning in Canberra, Australia, Carmen called the church twice before an answer;

'Hello,....Saint Francis Xavier Parish, this is Gwen'.

'Good morning Gwen, this is Carmen from the Civic Library. May I speak with Jeremy Ironside please'?

'Oh,..good morning, Carmen,..sorry but Father Irons is no longer our priest here, can I help you'?

'I hope so, Gwen, we have a rare book that Jeremy ordered some time back and has finally arrived, he has all ready paid for it but he did not leave a postal or delivery address, just this phone number'.

'Oh dear,...look the Archdiocese does not tell us where the priests go when they get promotional transfers and we have to direct any enquiries through them, if you just send it the the Diocese of Canberra and mark it for his attention, it should get to him'.

'I don't really know if I can do that, you see he has paid over five thousand dollars for this rare, collectors item book and I don't just want to send it to a generic address'.

'Oh wow, he loves his books, I know that much,...look....you did not get it from me but,....just two secs..it's here somewhere on my......stupid mobile..yes, The Presbytery at 41

Dargreaves Street, Bendigo. If you send it there he should definitely receive it'.

'Why thank you so much Gwen, I will get it away to him today, Thanks again, goodbye'.

'Well done Carmen, thank you very much', Nick said, 'Harry, find that number for the Bendigo Presbytery, it will be lunch time there and we'll get Carmen to do another call, but no book this time Carmen, tell them you are returning his call, it he answers just pretend its a wrong number, got it?'

Harry found the number and wrote in down for Carmen, she dialled.

'Presbytery, Robert speaking, may I help you', a very polished voice answered.

'Robert, this is Carmen, I am just returning a call from Jeremy, is he there please'?

'Father Ironside is no longer at this Presbytery Carmen, you will need to contact the Diocese, sorry goodbye'.

'Fuck it', said Harry, 'that's it'.

'Not at all, did you really think you would find him so easy, I have always had the opinion that priests are dumb, but not that fucking dumb, replied Nick., we will use the book idea, we will find him, get ready for a trip Harry'.

Nick and Harry had revisited the Telefónica shop and this time bought a 4g compact tracker with a sim card. This tracker, to extend battery life up to six months, could be turned on or off remotely with the telephone that it is paired to, simply by dialling the trackers sim card number and adding ##*, then turned off the same way but by adding #**.

An old relic of a book called The Five Saints of Spain that

they found in the village was used to carve out a neat fifteen by fifteen x seven millimetre crevice about three quarters of the way through the book and close to the spine, that way if somebody flipped through the pages of the book, the tracker would not be discovered. The book was then carefully placed in a suitable box and then in a padded post bag and then addressed to Father Jeremy Irons at the Presbytery in Bendigo, They had tested the tracker in and out of the packaging and had discovered that the signal was reading in the tens on the receiving scale and about four when in the package, this would allow Harry to know when the package had been opened.

This package was not placed in the mail though, this package was going to accompany Harry to Australia.

Harry had also needed to contact Colin Crisp, another Galaxy M24 was purchased and sent the same way as the Galaxy for Scott was sent.

'What the fuck are you up to now Harry', the voice of 'Crispy' echoed through Harry's Galaxy at one am on a Sunday morning,

'And I hope you are well to Col', Harry jested Col.

'I have a little unfinished business back in Oz and I need something light and quiet'.

'What sort of distance are you looking at Harry'?

'I would estimate ten metres max, but it needs to be a terminator, and...quiet'.

'The only thing that I have that might suit is a Margolin .22 target pistol, it's an auto 10 shot mag, it has a silencer and can fire a subsonic forty grain projectile at enough muzzle velocity to kill a big Rottweiler dog with one head shot and you won't hear a thing, you can upgrade the ammo to Winchester super x with twice the power and just a little muzzle blast noise, very faint actually'.

'Sounds good', said Harry, 'how can you deliver though, I will need it in Victoria'?

'There is a home brew shop at Frankston that does a twenty four hour collection for items using a locker system with an access code, I'll send you the code but you will need to pickup within twenty four hours of my call, so let me know prior'.

'You've got it Col', and they hung up. All sorted thought Harry and pretty easy so far.

'How do people ever live in Melbourne'? Harry thought to himself as he collected his hire car from the car park. He set the cars GPS for the Home Brew Store in Frankston, but before leaving the Melbourne city area he found a postal receiver and deposited his padded package. He then found the Home brew store and the contents of the locker, in the locker that Col had advised him

The Shamrock was a comfortable Hotel that Harry had stayed at before when he and his wife, Val, had visited friend's and Val's relatives in Country Victoria. There was a good bar and an excellent restaurant, the hotel was basically in the middle of the city and was an easy walk to other venues.

On day two of being in Bendigo, Harry assumed that the package would have been scanned by now and should be in transit so he dialled the trackers sim card and added ##* to turn it on, he then opened the scanners app on his mobile and after a few seconds the scanner was showing it's location on the app, it was showing the location to be 16 Deborah Street Bendigo. Harry checked the address and it showed it was the Bendigo mail centre. So the tracker had arrived in town, now he just had to wait for it to be delivered. 'You'r one smart cookie Nick', Harry was thinking as he headed to the restaurant for dinner.

The tracker had moved from Deborah Street to 41 Dargreaves Street the next day and had remained stationary inside the property and just to the left, it seemed inside the main entrance, for the next day. The package was then moved to number 47 Dargreaves Street and seemed to be to the far right of the building.

Harry thought he might call around to Dargreaves Street, doing the tourist thing and take a few pics and wander around. He was somewhat confused and needed to check out the lay of the land, as it were.

Number 41 Dargreaves Street, appeared to be a private residence. 'Hmm' thought Harry, wrong address and he drove on to number 47 Dargreaves Street, where the tracker was reporting as its location, this address also looked to be a private address. Harry checked the location again on his phone app and could not believe it, the package was now back at 16 Deborah Street, the mail centre.

After some consideration, Harry had concluded that the package was being redirected, Jeremy Irons was not in Bendigo. Harry's only course of action was to wait and watch where this tracker was going to from here.

Harry watched as the scanner went back to Melbourne and stayed there overnight, the next day it was out of range and remained so until late that evening and the location was Sydney Airport, the following morning it was still in Sydney but now at the suburb of Chullora where it remained for two days and then returned to the Sydney airport, the following morning the tracker was out mobile service until late in the evening when it arrived at Coffs Harbour. Harry was quite amazed how he could follow the tracker although he did become concerned when it showed that it was out of mobile service on a couple of occasions. It was a Sunday morning when the tracker finally left Coffs Harbour and started to travel south towards Kempsey, where it stayed overnight.

Monday morning and Harry checked the location before going down to breakfast, the tracker was at a small town beside the Macleay River called Scillons Flat.

Harry had waited, impatiently for another whole day to see if the package was still in transit or stationary. Harry had again checked it's location before going to bed, not only was the tracker still at Scillons Flat but the signal strength had increased by about thirty percent, indicting to Harry that the package had been opened, he assumed by Jeremy Irons.

Harry checked out of the hotel the following morning and had set his GPS from Bendigo to Scillons Flat, some 1260 kilometres. Harry had broken the trip up into roughly four hours driving each day and thoroughly enjoyed the trip and the hotels that he stayed at on the way, not to mention the different quality foods at the hotels, and the beers.

It was around five o clock when Harry finally pulled into Scillons Flat, population 3221, the sign had read.

He drove past the first motel, which he thought looked a

bit dilapidated, and drove on into the little village to see what else was on offer, nothing, not in the way of motels anyway but, the local pub looked tempting for a cold beer before he looked any further. It was a fairly large looking, typical two story pub, 'The Flat Hotel' it was simply called, painted white with federation green window sills, trims and corrugated iron roof it looked as though it was straight out of the past and walking into the bar was like going back at least a hundred years, if not more.

Harry walked up to the traditional looking timber bar with polished timber handrail and continuous stainless steel ashtray running along the bottom of the bar, a newer addition, maybe forty years ago he supposed, that also worked as a footrest and an ashtray.

'Good day, looks like you could handle a cold drink' asked the young lady behind the bar.

'I do believe you are correct Madam, a schooner of Carlton might be the plan' Harry replied whilst sitting on a bar stool and taking a look around the bar at the three seperate, lonely, drinkers.

The barmaid brought Harry's drink to him and Harry handed over a fifty dollar note, the barmaid rang up $8 on the till and returned his change.

'Is it a quiet day'? He asked.

'Normally a bit busier than this, never really know here, It could get busy around sixish', the barmaid replied.

'Whats the chance of a room for a few days'?

'No worries, it's $60 a night for a standard double room, or $75 for a queen room with ensuite'.

'I'll take a queen with the ensuite, thanks', Harry took his credit card out of his wallet and passed to the young lady, 'make it five nights please'.

She took Harry's credit card and disappeared into the next room to return a minute later with a key and an eftpos receipt. The key's label read '4'.

'The dining room opens at six this evening for dinner, if you like and also at six in the morning for breakfast, and believe me the food here is second to none' she said handing the key and the receipt to Harry.

'I'll vouch for that', one of the morbid looking drinkers at the bar said, 'the steaks are the best in NSW', he continued and now standing and moving towards Harry, 'Monty Graham, mate' he said now extending his arm towards Harry.

Harry shook his hand and said 'Harry Sutton'.

'What are you drinking Harry'? Monty asked putting a $50 on the bar.

'Schooner of Carlton, thanks Monty'.

'Are you here for long Harry'? Monty asked whilst holding his hand up and summoning the barmaid.

'Don't know yet, just looking around for somewhere to settle down'.

'Theres nothing around here Harry, not many people ever leave here once they arrive and get settled, the only place around here for sale is this pub'.

Monty's words struck Harry like a club, 'well' thought Harry, 'might be an idea'

'I didn't see any 'for sale' signs when I arrived'.

'Na, Sue reckons the 'for sale' signs will turn the customers away, not that there are many customers these days thanks to the local law man'.

'Sue'?

'The owner, you'll see her around shortly'.

'And how does the local copper keep the customers away' Harry asked inquisitively.

'He sits in his car, not the police car, his car, parked just up a bit from the pub and then swoops on anyone leaving the pub who's driving. He's a dead set arsehole'.

'Are you talking about my best friend again Monty'? Called out a graying, but attractive woman who had just entered the bar.

'G'day Sue, how are you doing, this is one of your guests, Harry' replied Monty.

'Hello Harry, I'm Sue, are you staying here? That's good, need all the guests I can get just now'. Sue responded.

Harry smiled and nodded as he said hello to Sue.

Harry enjoyed a few more beers with Monty, whom he had discovered was actually born here in Scillons Flat and lived on his five thousand acre property on his own since the death of his wife some seven years prior. Monty lives in the splendid homestead and leases two thousand acres of the land to a sheep farmer and three thousand acres to a cattle and horse breeder. Monty walks the one and a half kilometres from his home to the pub each afternoon for a few beers and dinner, then he walks home. Monty told Harry that he used to drive until the prick of a copper nailed him one evening.

The dining room at the pub was like going back in time with it's polished spotted gum floors and wainscoting panels around the walls to the chair rail mouldings and then semi gloss, white painted vertical tongue and groove timber from the high, ten foot (three metre) ceilings also of tongue and groove timbers, but painted in a more relaxing matt, off white finish and a polished spotted gum Scotia finish around it's perimeter, just beautiful, thought Harry.

Monty had invited himself to dine with Harry, and as he sat there looking at the menu, Harry could see that Monty had had a hard life, he had the appearance of a worker in days gone by and it now took it's toll on Monty's physique.

Harry had instantly like Monty upon meeting him in the bar, he had that sort of charisma that made you feel that you wanted to be in his circle.

'What sort of dollars would Sue be looking for in the hotel sale Monty', Harry asked.

'I have no idea old chap, I do know that they paid around the half million mark eight years ago, but they have done a lot to it'.

'They'?

'Yes, Sue and Brian, her husband, you won't get to meet him as he is in goal, thanks to our local copper. It's a bit of a story actually', Monty replied.

'I am all ears, old son', was Harry's response and Monty told Harry about Brian, that he and Sue had a panel beating business in Sydney somewhere and decided to sell up and move somewhere quieter and sort of semi retire. They found this pub on the market and came to have a look, fell in love with the pub and the area and the rest, as they say, is history. They were very busy renovating and painting and putting on special days for the patrons, all was going quite well until this prick of a copper started to stalk the patrons coming out of the pub at night and put the breathalyser on them resulting in people not coming to the pub, or not as many people, for drinks and meals. The pub started losing money and Sue and Brian were under financed, old story, so they had to do something to get the customers back.

Brian comes up with an idea and goes to Sydney to the Government surplus vehicle auctions and arrived back in town with a Volvo bus that was formally used to transport police around, a thirty nine seater. He had it resprayed and sign written with the pubs name and set up a time table to cover most of the town and ran it every hour from five thirty to midnight on Friday, Saturday and Sunday. All was going really good and the pub was packed every Friday through to Sunday until, the copper decides to pull Brian over in the bus one night to breathalyse him. Brian of course blew negative, but then the police constable claimed to observe some tablets in a plastic bag in the storage shelf near the side window, he immediately arrested Brian and got all of the passengers off the bus and called for back up from Coffs Harbour. Brian was taken to Coffs police station and the tablets were found to be MDMA (ecstasy) and Brian was charged with supplying and dealing, he was sentenced to ten years goal and the bus was confiscated as being a means to transport illicit drugs. Brian had never touched drugs in his life.

'Well fuck me', said Harry, he could not prevent his pommy accent from emerging, 'the rotten twat, he needs a fucking bullet'.

'That's why Sue is having to sell the pub' Monty concluded.

Harry had a lot of trouble trying to sleep that night, he knew he had a job on hand but he was thinking that buying this pub would be a good cover and maybe a good way to spend his retirement. It was two in the morning and Harry worked out that it would be just after midday in Mallorca Spain, he called Nick.

'Mate, how are you going' answered Nick, recognising the phone number, 'Don't tell me you'r not coming back'.

'I'll be coming back Nick, but not for a while yet, no dramas but just a couple of ideas that I want to pass over you'.

'And they would be'?

'Do have a million to go halves in a pub, might be cheaper that that, could be a neat little investment'?

'And the second thing is'?

'Knock a badge, not permanent, just so he gets wheels', Harry replied, knowing Nick would understand'.

'The second item should be easy enough , what state'? Nick needed to know.

'The first state', Harry said quoting the slogan on the NSW motor vehicle number plates.

'Piece of Piss Harry, you know how to get the details to me, but Harry, buying a fucking pub? Why the fuck would I want a fucking pub Harry'?

'It's only half a pub, I'm buying the other half, it'll work out Nick, if it does not then I'll buy you out'.

'Yeah, ok, just do it, tell me where to send the mil, the other bit will cost you around the fifty 'g' mark'.

'We'll be going halves in that too Nick, it's for the pubs sake'.

'You crack me up Harry, you really do' Nick was laughing, how did you go with the communion at church'?

'It will be fine, plenty of time for that, this pub could also work as a good cover for me'.

Harry turned off the light in his room and decided to talk to Sue in the morning and buy the pub.

Harry asked Sue what were the chances of a fillet steak for breakfast with an egg and tomatoes, tinned if possible and some chips. Sue had replied that it sounded just like a breakfast her husband Brian would order, less the tomatoes.

'Hope you enjoy, Harry', said Sue serving the breakfast.

'Do you have a few minutes for a chat Sue'?

'Yes, should be ok, I'll just get a coffee, would you like one Harry'?

Harry declined with the coffee and after a while Sue returned and sat opposite Harry.

'What price do you have on the hotel Sue'?

'The old Monty said you might be interested', Sue replied instantly with somewhat brighter eyes, 'nine hundred thousand plus stock, that should come in at about one hundred and fifty thousand, plus bits and pieces say one point one all up'.

Harry stopped eating and looked squarely at her, 'Sold' he said 'but I would want you to stay on and run it, at a good negotiated price of course and still live in here'.

Sue could not speak and could only mutter, 'are you serious and you haven't even seen the place yet, or the books'.

'I have seen something that I like, I was looking to buy a house around the area and I like this place and so be it. I am happy to stay in the room that I am in and you can remain in your residence'.

Harry finished his breakfast and continued to discuss the sale of the hotel with Sue who, by now was quite relieved and excited although somewhat sad that she had to sell the hotel, but she found it was getting harder and harder to satisfy the mortgage that she and her husband, Brian, had on the hotel as she now had to pay extra wages as Brian was no longer there to help, plus the downturn in patrons thanks to the arsehole copper.

Harry had told Sue that he was going into Coffs Harbour today to take back the hire car and organise another car for his transport and that he would also transfer the deposit for the hotel to her solicitor and that he would engage a solicitor for the conveyancing.

It was a pleasant one hour drive into Coffs Harbour from Scillons Flat, Port Macquarie is a little closer but lacked some of the facilities that Coffs could offer. He found the car hire company, dropped off the car and then walked to the main road that goes through Coffs and found the Coffs Harbour Subaru dealer who just happened to have an Outback turbo, demonstration model. Harry took the dealers details and the price of the car into the local branch of his bank and organised a bank cheque for his new Subaru Outback Turbo. Whilst at the bank Harry also organised the deposit for the purchase of the hotel to be transferred to Sue's solicitor, he also set up his account for internet banking and noted with delight that Nick's deposit of one million dollars had already been credited to his account.

Harry had then found a solicitor to act as conveyancer and also had an employment contract drawn up for both Sue and her husband, with a blank space where it stated remuneration.

On his way back into Scillons Flats he decided to visit the local, infamous, copper and pulled up in his new car in front of the police station and walked in knowing that it was most unlikely that face recognition camera's were employed in NSW police stations.

'Harry got quite a shock when he saw the young constable at the desk as he thought that there was only one officer at this station, and this officer looked much too young to be the 'famous' one, although he knew nothing of the country police station setups as when he was in the ACT police they only manned four police stations around the ACT and all had a crew of not less that thirty officers on duty.

'Good morning', Harry announced himself, 'are you the officer in charge'.

'Good morning sir, I am temporarily filling in, the acting sergeant is Bradley Moran but he is in Port Macquarie today, how can I help you'?

Harry introduced himself to the young constable and announced that he had just moved to the area and had just bought the 'Flat Hotel', to this the constable raised his eyebrows and said to Harry.

'Your'e kidding? We didn't even know it was for sale, Bradley will be pissed off' the young constable stated.

'It wasn't advertised, it was a private treaty, is there a problem'?

'Bradley has been sweating on that pub coming on to the market, that pub was his retirement plan' the young constable went on, volunteering more information than what he probably should.

'Oh', Harry replied, 'Will Bradley be back today'?

'Yeah, it's just his fortnightly staff meeting, he is generally back at around seven pm, they all normally have a couple of drinks following the meeting'.

This young copper was a treasure with his free information, Harry noted the day was Tuesday, hmm, good information. Harry told the constable that he would call in and see Bradley a bit later in the week and said 'Good day'.

Back at the hotel, Harry found Sue and told her that he had paid the deposit, which she already knew, he also told her that he had instructed his solicitor to proceed with a settlement as soon as practicable to both parties as he had the cash to make settlement. Sue was beside herself and even happier when Harry told her about the work contract that he had prepared for both her and Brian, as, he said you never know, Brian just might get an early release.

Sue had then apologised to Harry saying that they had moved him from room number four to room number one as that room was much bigger as it had two bedrooms and an a lounge. Perfect Harry had replied and then asked if there was a lock up garage that was available for him as well, which it was, plus a private office was also available.

Things for proceeding smoothly for both the hotel

transition and Harry's plans, Harry had just walked into the drive through bottle department when a police landcruiser drove in, the police driver exited the vehicle and approached the sales counter, the police officer, a senior constable, identified Harry as a new face and assumed him to be the new owner and called out to him.

'Are you the new owner'?

'Almost, as good as all done' responded Harry.

'Acting sergeant Bradley Moran' the officer said approaching Harry with his hand outstretched.

'Harry Sutton', Harry replied, ignoring the police officers hand.

Meanwhile the barmaid, who also kept her eye on the bottle department, had been getting a carton of Tooheys Dry Lager from the cool room and had passed it to Bradley Moran, who in turn had placed it inside his vehicle left hand side back door, he then proceeded to get back into the drivers side door when Harry spoke.

'You have forgotten to pay for the carton of beer, acting sergeant'.

'Sue will explain it to you', the officer smirked towards Harry.

'I don't think so, the stock has all been transferred and I have paid for it, that is my beer and if you wish to take it with you, then you need to pay for it'.

Acting sergeant Moran, got back out of his car and approached Harry. Harry regarded Moran as a weedy looking specimen to be a member of the police force, unlike his days when a height and weight requirement kept shit like this out of the service.

'You need to learn Sutton, that I run this town and in return and out of respect many business owners offer me gratitude in the form of small gifts', the acting sergeant was becoming annoyed.

'You'll get no gratification in the way of gifts from me, you either pay for the carton of beer, or hand it back and if you don't I shall report you', said Harry as he pulled his mobile phone from his pocket and started to dial 000.

The astonished acting sergeant was now clearly becoming wild and turned back towards the rear passenger door and withdrew the carton of beer and threw it onto the ground beside the sales counter, smashing the contents.

Using his mobile phone that was already in his hand, Harry simply took a photograph of the scene which included the acting sergeant, the police car and the smashed carton. He then calmly told the officer to get off the premises and don't come back, Harry then took a video of the police car smoking up it's tyres as it accelerated out of the bottle shop driveway.

Harry immediately looked up the email address for the NSW police media and issues, public affairs branch and forwarded the photograph and the video with a full explanation of both, together with a formal complaint.

'Round one' Harry said to no one in particular.

Once Sue had heard about the bottle shop incident she became concerned and spoke to Harry and told him to be careful. He had responded and reassured her that there was nothing to worry about, 'you don't just keep stepping over weeds in the garden, they become annoying, so you simply remove them', he told her.

It was just about two weeks since Harry had decided to buy the pub from Sue that sensational news was broadcast from all the major television station's on the Wednesday evening news.

It stated; *The two major NSW newspapers received a tape recording of a full confession from a police officer in relation to false drug charges of a hotel co owner, the tape revealed how the police officer had used drugs that he had taken from the evidence safe of a different case and planted them on a bus that the accused was driving at the time. The news report went on to say that the officer involved had claimed that he had arrived back from police matters in the nearby town of Port Macquarie and when alighting from his police vehicle at his home he was seized by at least two men who placed a head cover over him and strapped both of his arm's around his body making him totally immobile. He was then forced, through excessive violence causing great pain to make the verbal statement on an audio tape. He was then held captive for about 24 hrs until the tape was made available to police and the press. Although the officer has stated that he made the statement under extreme duress and had also falsified the statement in an effort to be set free, police have confirmed that evidence, that is very similar, to that used in the hotel owners case, is missing from another case.*

It is further reported that the officer received extensive injuries to both of his knee's and may not be able to return to normal activities.

The following Friday morning, just two days after the

spectacular news report, Brian Huntley was released from prison and Bradley Moran was charged with various, serious charges that would see him serve a lengthy term in prison, he is now also confined to a wheel chair resulting from injuries from his alleged attackers.

The Bradley Moran story is now emerging right across Australia as a warning to corrupt police officers as it seemed that a well trained team of experts may have been responsible for the Moran abduction and it should not be ruled out that it won't happen again.

That Saturday, all weekend for that matter, was a very joyous occasion around the pub, the bus had been returned on the same day that Brian was released and a casual driver had been engaged to drive the old weekend roster to collect and drop off the pub patrons who could also join in Brian's home coming celebrations.

Many patrons also drove their cars to the pub and were very mindful of how many drinks they could have, but at least they knew that they would no longer be subject to a breathalyser that would include vehicle checks, or so they hoped.

Harry got on well with Brian, who was about a similar age to him, they were both very thankful for Harry taking over the pub and having them run it for him and at a generous remuneration.

Both Sue and Brian were convinced that Harry had a hand in the demise of Bradley Moran as Sue had first hand information about what had happened in the drive through bottle shop and knew that Harry had filed a formal complaint against Moran. Harry had not quite denied any involvement but had also claimed his innocence, but when they asked Harry how they could possibly repay him, he did say that he may be in need of a favour one day.

Harry had been maintaining his grey beard and his shaved head and had now bought a collar length grey wig online. He had been a resident in Scillons Flat for almost three months and was settling in, he had also been attending Sunday mass at the Sisters of Mercy Parish in Scillons Flat. Harry had been making it a habit for the last month or so to take the worn pathway from the pubs beer garden across a vacant block of land to the main shopping centre of Scillons Flat.

This path led past the rear of the the parish church and Harry had actually made contact with Father Michael Wright, the local priest of the Scillons Flat Parish on a number of occasions and had no problems with taking several photographs of the good priest, unbeknown to him of course. He had also witnessed the priest signing a reference for a fellow parish member with his left hand.

These photo's were sent back to Nick in Spain who forwarded them to Harry's son Scott, with a letter asking for positive identification of the photographs to be that of Jeremy Irons. The confirmation that the photographs were definitely that of Jeremy Ironside eventually came back to Harry, via Nick in Spain.

So, not only had the church made a cover up of the reports of child molestation in respect to Father Ironside and relocated him, but they had also changed his name to Michael Wright.

The town of Scillons Flat has a population of approximately

3221 according to its last census, it had two hotels, 'The Flat Hotel' and the 'Scillons Flat Hotel'. The latter burnt to the ground in the early 2000's and was never rebuilt.

There are two motels at Scillons Flat, an IGA supermarket, two butcher shops, two ladies hairdressers, one chemist, one newsagent, one fish and chips shop, one Chinese cafe, called Happy's (how did you guess) and course the Post Office. Education consisted only of a public primary school, Catholic children travelled the twenty odd kilometres

into Kempsey as with the high school aged children.

Other than the Sisters of Mercy parish church was the Anglican Church of all Saints. It was an idealist retirement village where nothing really happens, or very rarely. The confessional at the parish church was open only on each Saturday between seven pm and eight pm.

Wearing his new wig and a pair of disposable kitchen gloves, Harry had arrived at the church at seven thirty on the Saturday night to find it empty and had gone into the confessional, it did not take long until Harry could hear the priest entering the other side.

'Welcome and may God, who has enlightened every heart, help you to know your sins and trust in his mercy'. Said the priest. Harry was hoping to God that it was Irons as the voice was a little muffled coming through the grill.

'Amen' said Harry, 'Bless me, Father, for I have sinned. It has been ten weeks since my last confession'.

Harry then pushed the rolled up document through the grill of the confessional to the priests side and said,

'Father you need to read this and then sign it, or you will be meeting your maker this evening'.

Harry stormed from his side of the confessional door and into the priest side of the confessional door with the Margolin target pistol in his hand, he took aim at the priest,

'Jeremy Ironside, sign that confession or I will shoot you dead' said Harry to a shaking, almost hysterical priest who was in no condition to read the document.

'Here, sign it now' prompted Harry passing a biro to the priest who was like he was about to pass out, he took the biro from Harry and without taking his eyes off Harry, he signed the document, Harry leaned down and placed the muzzle of the silenced Margolin into the priest's ear and pulled the trigger.

The priest seemed to collapse to the floor before the almost soundless hiss report of the Margolin was heard, the priest made no noise as he fell but the chair clattered quite loudly. Harry quickly placed the Margolin into the lifeless left hand of the priest and carefully moved the fallen document out of the path of the blood that now streamed from the priest's head. Harry exited the confessional and closed both of its doors, the church was empty as he left and returned in the dark to the pub, once there he removed his wig and went directly behind the public bar.

'Sorry about that fellow's but I had to take that leak', Harry said, 'who's next'.

The news of the local police sergeant had made Scillons Flat famous as far as news went and for about a week following the revelations of the made up drug charges and the assault on the corrupt police officer. Just as the town was getting back to normal, the next Monday morning it made national headlines again.

'Scillons Flat Priest found dead in church clutching signed confession'!

The report stated that the police at this stage did not suspect any foul play and it appeared he was actually assuming a fictitious name as Father Michael Wright. Although police did not release the contents of the confession, leaked sources would indicate that he was being shielded by the church from charges relating to acts of child molestation at a church in a Canberra suburb.

This time the news reports failed to bring a caravan of reporters as it did with the Bradley Moran saga and the town soon settled down, a new priest was installed within a matter of days and Harry resumed his visits for Sunday mass and joined the other members of the congregation in pointing at the confessional and whispering what they had heard and that the word was out that it should be a warning to other priests that the lord works in mysterious ways.

Things were going very well at the pub, 'just like it used to be' said many of the locals who were sometimes three deep at the bar and there always seemed to be a packed carpark. A new police sergeant had been installed in town and he was busy assisting the police special investigations team that had been sent up from Sydney in relation to Bradley Moran.

Harry Sutton decided that it was time for him to retire and enjoy his pub, he couldn't wait for Nick to come over for a visit, but that will be a little while yet.

'Good morning Harry' said Sue as Harry went into breakfast, 'don't forget we have the live jazz on this weekend'.

'No, I won't forget, I am really looking forward to this, especially to see how it goes, if it works we'll do something similar every week', Harry's mobile interrupted him, 'sorry Sue', he said as he answered his phone.

'No worries Aitch, I'll get your breakfast' replied Sue knowing full well that he would have a steak and chips with eggs and tinned tomatoes for his 'usual' breakfast.

'Sorry to get you out of bed mate' was the reply.

'It's nine o'clock mate, of course, I'm out of bed, who is this'?

'Your fucking partner, dickhead, can you come and get me from the airport'.

'Nick?.....you are kidding me, where are you?

'Coffs airport mate, when you are ready!' Nick replied, 'no rush, I expect it will take you an hour or so to get here, I'll wander around and find a pub for lunch, give me a call on this number when you get here'.

Harry told Sue to cancel brekky as he had to go to Coffs and he went upstairs to his room to get his car keys, he came back down and was out of the back door heading to his car when he suddenly had a thought and returned to the dining room looking for Sue.

'Sue!.......Sue!, are you still here'?

'I'm in here Harry, eating your breakfast'.

'We will need another room tonight for a mate of mine.'

'For tonight and tomorrow is fine, but we are booked up for the weekend Harry.'

Harry nodded OK and went back outside to get his car and head off to Coffs Harbour. He was quite excited that Nick had finally decided to come and have a look at their pub and a hundred questions were going through his mind.

It was ten forty five when Harry got into Coffs after getting stuck behind trucks and road works, he pulled over to the side of the road and looked at his mobile for the last call and pushed 'dial'.

'I'm at a place called the 'Green Horse' tavern Harry, I haven't a clue where it is really, but it's on a busy road.'

'I'll find it, see you soon.'

Harry found the tavern about ten minutes after hanging up the phone and he walked into the public bar, and looked around at the dozen or so people that were in there, no Nick. Harry saw a sign that said 'thru to bistro', but still no Nick and hardly anyone in there, he looked around more and found the gaming room, but no Nick., 'Maybe he is having a leak' Harry thought as he walked back to the public bar.

He sat on a stool near the bar and took out his phone and redialled the last number, it started to ring and Harry could hear a 'Bohemian Rhapsody' ringtone somewhere behind him and he turned around.

'Here,...dickhead' called a familiar voice from a total bald headed and bearded stranger wearing coke bottle glasses and giving Harry the 'bird' with his centre finger on his right hand.

'No way, ...no fucking way, fuck me, how the fuck are you Nick' Harry could not believe Nick's appearance.

'It's 'Mick' Harry,..' Mick', Mick Marsh, responded a

totally different looking Nick. 'Two more schooners of Carlton, thanks love' he said to the girl behind the bar.'I did a Skassie Harry, just like you.

'Well, it's good to see you...er, Mick' Said Harry picking up his beer from the bar, 'how long are you here for?'

'Couple of days here, then up to Brissy for a week or so, got a little job to do, I'll tell you about it later, Cheers!'

On the drive back to Scillons Flat, Nick told Harry how easy it was to change his identity and come back to Australia. He had placed all his assets, which included his home on the Island and his bank accounts to his various brothers. The reason he was back was to assist three of his cousins who are roof tilers around Brisbane and was hoping that Harry might be able to assist.

'I am not quite sure how I could assist Nick,..sorry Mick, I am too old to do any roof tiling' Harry stated.

'No, no tiling required,' Nick Laughed, 'just need a building surveyor, a QBSA inspector, that is, a fake QBSA building inspector', Nick then went on to explain the situation with his cousins.

They have supplied and installed the roof tiles on three unit blocks in Rockhampton, around five thousand square meters and they went in at $155 m^2, $775,000 for the whole project which was about $250,00 for each unit block.

They completed the first block and submitted their account for that and started on the second block, they had almost finished the second block and they had still not been paid for the first block so they gave the builder twenty four hours to pay for the first block or they would stop work.

'At this stage', said Nick they had already paid for the tiles for the first two blocks which was around forty five dollars per square metre,so around one hundred and fifty grand out of pocket plus the cost of labour which was about the same value again, say three hundred thousand dollars they had put out and the builder had not paid within the twenty four hours, so they stopped work until the builder came good with the money

The builder threatened them with a clause in their contract that basically stated, that if they failed to complete their contract, then the builder could bring in another contractor to complete the works at the expense of the original contractor. And that is what he did for the balance of the second block of about thirty per cent and the third block at 100 per cent,' Nick went on to say, 'The builder back charged my boys with the cost of the replacement tiler who happened to be two hundred and seventeen dollars per square metre, that is forty five per cent more of their original price. For the part of the second unit and all of the third unit, plus liquidated damages for lost time, less the work that they had completed, my boy's bill from the builder was a total of two hundred and fifty thousand dollars.'

'And all legal,' added Harry, 'your boys, they signed the contract which had that, fairly standard clause, that they should have been aware of and it was your boys that stopped work on the job, so the sneaky builder took advantage of that clause and turned your boys project into a loss of two hundred and fifty grand, what a bastard he must be'.

'It wasn't just my boys, Harry, he did a similar thing with some of the other trades as well on this and other projects'.

'It does stink, Nick and sadly the builder has the law behind him through the legitimate, but scandalous acting, contract', Harry stated and then said, 'What do you have in mind for this builder, Nick?'

Nick passed a Queensland Building Services Authority identification card across to Harry as he was driving, a quick glance at it showed a photograph in the top right hand corner of the card, of Harry wearing thick rimmed glasses.

'Hmmm' said Harry, 'from our friend 'Chrispy' no doubt, and the plan?'

Nick was pretty stoked when he saw the pub, he couldn't believe that they had bought it so cheaply and he shuddered when he thought that the copper who was sending the previous owners slowly broke, had intentions of buying the pub for even less.

Sue had placed Nick in room three for the next two nights and Harry had told her that he and Nick would be leaving on Friday morning but returning possibly the next Friday so as to keep the room for Nick.

The next day, Thursday, was a catch up day for both Nick and Harry and many beers were enjoyed, they had planned to drive up to Brisbane on Friday morning and then to Rockhampton on Saturday with a meeting of Nick's cousins on Sunday, a busy weekend coming up.

It was an uneventful trip to Brisbane of some six hours and we stayed at the Casino in the old treasury building. After good entertainment and good food we had an early night for the trip to Rockhampton.

Nick's cousins seemed to be extensions of Nick, all Russians must be of solid build judging by these fellows, Aleksandr was the eldest of the four Romeril brothers then Mikhail, Bogdan and Radimir, Nick called them all by nicknames after he had introduced me to them. Alex, Mick, Dan and Dimmy.

The builder, John Jeffries had been sent an email on the previous Friday morning with a forged heading of the Queensland Building Services Authority and also with a fictitious return address which returned a response to Alex. The email had requested an inspection of a section of tiled roofing in the company of the tiling contractor and the builder for the following Monday morning at ten thirty am.

Harry was the QBSA representative and he met with John Jeffries on the Monday morning at ten thirty, normally Jeffries's building supervisor would handle this type of random inspection but he was enjoying a day off and had gone fishing with one of his friends, who just happened to be Mick Romeril.

Harry had gone into the site office and introduced himself to a very agitated and somewhat entitled John Jeffries who responded to Harry with.

'Haven't you blokes got anything to do, fucking me around like this'?

Harry simply replied, 'Where is the tiling contractor'?

'He should be out there organising the scissor lift, I hope, let's go'.

Harry and Jeffries went around to the first unit block and found Alex and Danny with the scissor lift that was set up next to a six metre rubbish hopper, Dimmy was near the hopper collecting pieces of broken roof tiles and throwing them in the hopper. There was no one else present on this site as it was almost complete.

Harry and Jeffries put on safety harnesses and joined Alex and Danny on the scissor lift, Harry got on before Jeffries, as they had previously planned and they clipped their safety lines to the scissor lift then Jeffries closed and locked the entry door as he was the last one in and standing next to the door. Alex pulled the elevate lever and they rose the four stories, approximately fourteen metres to the roof level.

Unbeknown to Jeffries, as he was glancing across the site, Danny and Alex had changed places with Harry and were now standing next to Jeffries, Danny quietly unclipped Jeffries's safety line and as he did so, Alex reached across and unlocked, then pushed open the door resulting in Jeffries falling from the scissor lift. Alex lowered the scissor lift and let Harry off the scissor lift, Harry immediately proceeded to his car and left the site. Alex called triple zero and asked for an ambulance, he then moved the scissor lift to the other side of the rubbish hopper with the scissor lift door in the opposite direction of the hopper giving the impression that Jeffries had fallen from the roof, he went to the rubbish hopper where Jeffries lay, the broken tiles had made Jeffries landing far worse and were most likely a contributor to his death. Dimmy had climbed into the hopper, removed Jeffries's mobile phone from his pocket and deleted the bogus email from the QBSA. The three brothers waited for the ambulance to arrive.

The three brothers had each made sworn statements to the Workplace Health and Safety officers who attended the accident site. Each statement read precisely the same, Jeffries had called them to rectify a defect in the tiling and had taken them up onto the roof to show them, everyone had connected their safety lines to the roof anchors, but it seemed, except for Jeffries who slipped on the tiled roof. The brothers expressed their grief of losing a workmate and friend.

The building project was placed into the hands of receivers and administrators were appointed, a complete site safety audit was carried out as was a complete contract audit that revealed some illegal contract variations that resulted in the Romeril brothers being paid all of their contractual commitments from Jeffries's now defunct company, as with some other contractors.

It was also revealed that Jeffries's building licence had been cancelled by the QBSA two years prior to him commencing this unit project, this resulted in an internal audit of the QBSA.

Weekdays were slow and easy for both Nick and Harry at the pub, weekends, however, were hectic, but fun.

'How long do you intend to stay here, Harry' asked Nick.

'Probably forever Nick, I think it's time to retire, and you'?

'Yeah, it's a pretty good lifestyle here, I'll probably stay until something comes up' said Nick just as his mobile phone rang. 'What.....you are fucking kidding me,...Mate...I'll grab Harry and we'll be right down there.

'Plenty of time to retire down the track, I suppose' thought Harry.